SPECTRUM 25

THE BEST IN CONTEMPORARY FANTASTIC ART

SPECTRUM 25

THE BEST IN CONTEMPORARY FANTASTIC ART

EDITED BY JOHN FLESKES

FLESK

Previous spread: Beowulf's Battle by William O'Connor. Above: Tintinnabula: Trees by Rovina Cai

Edited and designed by John Fleskes.
Copyedited by Martin Timins.
Book production, plus design and editing assistance by Katherine Chu.

First Printing, November 2018. Printed in Hong Kong.
Paperback edition ISBN: 978-1-64041-006-0
Hardcover edition ISBN: 978-1-64041-007-7

Artists, art directors and publishers interested in receiving entry information for the next *Spectrum* competition can visit *spectrumfantasticart.com* for details. "Call for Entries" posters (which contain complete rules and lists of fees for participation) are mailed in October each year.

A special thank you to Katherine Chu for her assistance in researching material for the Year in Review, her role in running the Spectrum Awards Ceremony, and for her tireless efforts to manage the Flesk offices.

Cover artwork: "Mittlander" by Paul Bonner
Back cover artwork: "A Girl & Her Friends" by Wesley Burt

flesk publications.com
spectrumfantasticart.com
spectrumfantasticartlive.com

CONTENTS

SPECTRUM 25 CALL FOR ENTRIES POSTER BY SCOTT GUSTAFSON

Seattle

The *Spectrum* 25 jury from left to right: Chuck Pyle, Tyler Jacobson,
Karla Ortiz, and Tran Nguyen. Photo by John Fleskes

SPECTRUM 25 JUDGING EVENT

The *Spectrum* 25 judging event was held on February 24, 2018, at the
Flesk Publications offices in Santa Cruz, California. We were honored
to host this year's distinguished group of judges, which consisted of Terry
Dodson, Tyler Jacobson, Tran Nguyen, Karla Ortiz and Chuck Pyle.
These individuals are currently playing a significant role in setting the
tone of artistic excellence for the future while paving the way for a better
community for our next generation. They are bringing forth imagery that
defines today's fantastic-art genre while also helping others to navigate the
terrains of the industry through unparalleled guidance.

    These five jury members combined their expertise, professionalism and
knowledge to help make the difficult decisions when selecting among the
many submitted entries for *Spectrum* 25. Each judge votes anonymously
while reviewing the submissions. A vote of three or more secures a work of
art for inclusion in the book. Once this initial stage is complete, the judges
work as a team to select the five nominees along with the silver and gold
recipients in each of the eight categories.

    The five jelled immediately upon their arrival. This type of camaraderie
makes for a unique and special *Spectrum* annual each year. Bringing a
jury together to discuss the merits of the art as a team is one of the ways
we place the community and relationships at the forefront of all that we
do. We greatly appreciate these judges for their respective time and
experience, along with everyone who submitted art.

TERRY DODSON

*"Being a judge for Spectrum 25 was a fantastic experience and humbling
to work alongside the other judges. It was overwhelming to see so much
great artwork but also a terrific learning experience to be able to 'look' at
so much artwork critically in so short an amount of time—a couple of terms
of art education in a few hours!"*

Oregon-based Terry Dodson has been a professional artist since 1993.
He has worked on such comics and characters as *Harley Quinn*, *Spider-Man*, *Star Wars*, *Superman*, *Wonder Woman*, the *X-Men*, *Harry Potter*
and *The Avengers*. His clients have included Lucasfilm, Riot Games,
Hasbro, Mattel, DC Entertainment, Warner Brothers, ESPN, Electronic
Arts, Hanna-Barbara, Marvel Entertainment, Sideshow Collectibles and
many more. Dodson currently is working with writer Xavier Dorison on
Red One, his own graphic-novel series for Image Comics, and with writer
Matt Fraction on the upcoming comics title *Adventureman!* He remains
a popular artist in the industry, a status he attributes in large part to the
contributions of his wife, Rachel, who adds her masterly inking to his work.

Jace, Unraveler of Secrets
Art for Magic: The Gathering

Thrice By Twilight
"Swank" exhibition, 2017

TYLER JACOBSON

"Judging for Spectrum 25 was an incredible experience. It was truly inspirational to see such a volume of beautiful artwork and to have the opportunity to discuss it with a panel of artists for whom I have great respect and admiration. Working alongside Chuck, Tran, Karla and Terry was wonderful. I want to express my deepest gratitude to John Fleskes and Kathy Chu for making all this happen. Spectrum has always been an important community for me, and I am so glad such fantastic people are fostering it into the future."

Tyler Jacobson is an illustrator working out of the Pacific Northwest. He graduated from the Academy of Art University in San Francisco in 2009 with a degree in illustration. Having always been driven toward sci-fi/fantasy art, he soon began working for the game industry as a freelance artist. He has been creating illustrations and concept art for Dungeons & Dragons since 2009 and designing card illustrations and concept art for Magic: The Gathering since 2012. Over the years Jacobson has painted illustrations for various companies and publishers, including Paizo Publishing, *Texas Monthly*, Marvel Entertainment, Adult Swim, Konami, The Penguin Group, *Rolling Stone* magazine, Toyota, *Men's Journal*, Tor Books, *Scientific American*, *Entertainment Weekly*, *The New Yorker* and *Sports Illustrated*. His prizes include the Spectrum 19 Gold Award for Advertising, the Spectrum 23 Gold Award for Institutional, the Society of Illustrators LA Illustration West 52 Silver Award for Book Cover ands the Joseph Morgan Henninger Award for Best in Show.

TRAN NGUYEN

"Being part of this year's jury has been a one-of-a-kind experience! Seeing the inner workings of Spectrum and getting to gawk at the thousands and thousands of gorgeous entries alongside my ridiculously amicable jurors has been a treasure for me. It's going to be a sensational book!"

Tran Nguyen is an award-winning illustrator, gallery artist and muralist. She received her BFA in illustration at Savannah College of Art & Design in 2009. Born in Vietnam and raised in the States, she is fascinated by creating visuals in the realm of fantasy and surrealism. Her achieves a soft, delicate quality in her artworks using colored pencils and acrylics on paper.

Ultimum
Chimerical, Spoke Art Gallery, 2016

A Diet of Treacle
Paperback book cover for Lawrence Block's crime fiction novel

KARLA ORTIZ

"Being a judge for Spectrum was a very eye-opening experience for me. It felt like I got to peek behind the curtain on what it actually takes to be in such an important book. Thousands of entries, and only about eight or nine percent actually make it in! That in itself is quite a miracle. However, for me, the true joy was to see all the very different distinct artistic voices. So many members of the community coming together to showcase their work! It's immensely inspiring to see the best of the industry alongside the future of the industry! This was a wonderful experience, and it gives me a new profound respect for the care the book takes in order to curate its pages."

Karla Ortiz is an internationally recognized award-winning artist from Puerto Rico. With her exceptional design sense, realistic rendering and character-driven narratives, Ortiz has contributed to many big-budget films, including *Jurassic World, World of Warcraft, Rogue One: A Star Wars Story,* Marvel's *Thor: Ragnarok, Black Panther, Infinity Wars* and, most notably, her design of Doctor Strange for Marvel's *Doctor Strange.* Her work is also recognized in the fine-art world, showcasing her figurative and mysterious art in notable galleries such as Spoke Art and Hashimoto Contemporary in San Francisco, Nucleus Gallery and Thinkspace in LA and Galerie Arludik in Paris. Ortiz currently lives in San Francisco with her cat, Budy.

CHUCK PYLE

"It was an extraordinary honor to be chosen to help select 'the best among the best' from among so many worthy submissions by so many passionate and professional artists. It proves, again, that conceptual, narrative art is a vitally alive market, and the judges I was humbled to be on the same panel with are in and of themselves 'the best among the best.'"

Chuck Pyle's realistic style was inspired by the likes of Norman Rockwell, N.C. Wyeth and John Singer Sargent. His paintings have been widely exhibited and are part of many private and institutional collections. Pyle has been commissioned to create illustrations, paintings and cartoons for clients and executives at AT&T, United Airlines, Viansa Winery, the United States Air Force, the National Park Service, Nisshin Foods of Japan, Penguin Books, *The Saturday Evening Post, The New York Times,* Politico, *The Atlantic Monthly* and *The Boston Globe.* He is represented in New York by Lindgren & Smith and in the Bay Area by Linda Demoreta. As a founding participant in Sonoma Plein Air and Telluride Plein Air, Pyle actively promotes outdoor painting and has taught plein-air painting in Umbria and Florence, Italy, for the Academy of Art University.

Pyle is currently the director of the School of Illustration at the Academy of Art University in San Francisco, where he earned the Distinguished Alumnus Award and in 2017 received an honorary doctorate. He also was awarded the Distinguished Educator in the Arts Award by the Society of Illustrators in 2015. He teaches drawing and illustration and also mentors the next generation of artists and visual storytellers. Pyle has been a Petaluman since 1989 and is married to Tina Hittenberger. He is the proud "Bonus Dad" of her two children, Clarke and Lauren.

CLAIRE WENDLING
SPECTRUM GRAND MASTER
by Arnie Fenner

"When I was growing up, I wished I could draw with the power of Jack Kirby or Frank Frazetta," the late Rocketeer creator Dave Stevens once said. *"But when I was an adult and had been working for a while, I wished I could draw with the heart of Claire Wendling."*

Dave wasn't—and isn't—alone.

It's tempting to think of Claire Wendling as something of a wunderkind or prodigy and, considering the speed with which she achieved international recognition, it's perfectly understandable to do so. She has described her childhood in southern France as someone who grew up often alone, "talking to plants and with a pencil as a best friend." And it was that "best friend" who helped Claire channel her creative energy and embark on a lifelong journey of imagination.

In 1989, while still in art school at the École des Beaux-Arts, she was presented with the prestigious "Artist of the Future" prize at the Angouleme Comics Festival. Claire showed that the honor wasn't a fluke the next year, when she launched the comics series *Lumières de l'Amalou (Lights of the Amalou)* with writer Christophe Gibelin. The first volume was recognized at Angouleme, this time with its Press Award in 1991. Two years later, Claire was honored with the Best Young Illustrator prize for her covers for Player One magazine. Something of an artistic chameleon, her work covered a lot of stylistic ground—from loose, spontaneous drawings to impressionistic paintings to highly detailed renderings. She tackled any subject matter with confidence and compassion, whether it was erotica or sword & sorcery or whimsical fantasies. And if you want to talk *personality*… Well! Claire's barbarians, nymphs, animals, monsters and superheroes literally leaped off the page and convinced viewers of their reality.

It was inevitable that others took notice of the buzz surrounding this hot young artist: In 1997 she was hired by Warner Brothers and moved to California to work on various animation projects, including *The Quest for Camelot*. But Los Angeles didn't turn out to be quite her cup of tea, and Claire returned to France eight months later. She then published *Desk*, an energetic collection of sketches made while living in L.A., as a way to chronicle her experiences. (An English-language version was later published by Stuart Ng Books.) More comfortable creating in her home studio, Claire worked long-distance for a wide variety of international clients; in her spare time, she self-published collections of her sketches and drawings.

There are many qualities that make a Spectrum Grand Master, and one of them is perseverance: Claire's was severely tested when she faced a host of life-threatening health problems. For nearly five years, her art career was put on hold as she focused all her energies on getting well—and when she came out on the other side, she found she had to literally start over and relearn everything she knew about drawing. Claire began by sketching outdoors. She went to cafés with a sketchpad, trying to remember the process and relearning to draw intuitively without a lot of preplanning. And with patience and diligence, her skills returned.

Of *course* they did: She's Claire Wendling, after all.

Fellow Spectrum Grand Master Iain McCaig presented Claire with the award at the conclusion of the *Spectrum 25* ceremony at the historic Brookledge Theater in Los Angeles on May 5, 2018. He read Claire's acceptance speech to an enthusiastic audience:

"Dear artists and arts lovers, you can't imagine how much you make me happy and proud—and humble as well—to be accepted as one of you with this award.

It's as much an honor as it is a responsibility for me. I remember quite a long time ago as a young French artist with studio mates when we were buying every imported *Spectrum* book we could find, in awe and full of the dream to be part of this world—the one of the recognized and super-talented artists from overseas! Your books and your works allowed us to discover many artists we wouldn't have had a clue about… In a few words, it seemed a wonderful and unreachable world for us. I still have those books! Imagine my surprise when John Fleskes asked me three years ago to do the annual "call for entries" poster! I didn't show John many emotions then, but everything in me was both smiling and crying at the same time, remembering how important *Spectrum* had been to me growing up. I thought my journey with *Spectrum* couldn't bring me more happiness than that, but now you come—out of the blue—with this honor. In a way, it's fortunate I'm not present tonight: I would cry more than talk! Thank you so, so much!"

Though Claire is a bit amazed and genuinely humbled by her stature in the arts community, neither the attention she received early in her career nor her being honored with the Spectrum Grand Master Award nearly thirty years later is surprising. Whether working as a comic artist, game designer, illustrator or concept artist, she has *always* had the unique ability to excel and to make any subject matter—any assignment—her own. Claire has explained, simply, "I draw because I draw."

We are all enriched because she does.

Raven

MIRANDA MEEKS
SPECTRUM RISING STAR

"It's an incredible honor to be the recipient of such a distinguished award! I can only thank my friends and family for being so supportive of my career, and I express my gratitude to this amazing community of artists. Thank you for inspiring me and for being so welcoming and inclusive."

The Spectrum Rising Star Award recognizes and acknowledges an emerging artist who demonstrates exceptional abilities and dedication in the fantastic-art arena. It also intends to encourage all newcomers to stay focused on their work and to persevere through the challenges they will face in building a career in the creative arts.

The nominees for this year's Rising Star Award were chosen by John Fleskes, Colin and Kristine Poole, and Dan dos Santos. The ultimate winner, Miranda Meeks, was selected by the Pooles—the Rising Star creators—and announced during the Spectrum 25 awards ceremony on May 5, 2018, at the Brookledge Theater in Los Angeles.

Miranda Meeks is a professional illustrator known for her haunting and ethereal digital illustrations. The primary focus of her work centers around the idea that beauty and darkness can weave together to form an intriguing narrative. She captures moments of stillness and silence, often evoking a melancholic mood or a feeling of subtle tension. Depicting women of strength is a recurring theme, as Meeks strives to present images that empower other women and girls to feel that same sense of strength. Soft, overcast lighting, fluid elements and delicate gradients are also featured prominently in her work, which intensifies the atmosphere of otherworldliness and solitude.

Inspired by darker films from directors such as Tim Burton and M. Night Shyamalan, Meeks seeks outside sources of creativity that convey similar themes of darkness and soft beauty. In elementary school, she discovered the picture book The Mysteries of Harris Burdick by Chris Van Allsburg. The tales that accompanied the enigmatic pictures influenced her perception of how stories can be told and continue to influence her work today. She also finds inspiration from other fields like graphic design and fine art, which she threads back into her own work.

YEAR IN REVIEW
by JOHN FLESKES

Spectrum's core message of community was at the forefront of its mission statement well before it was first published. The initial idea to launch Spectrum was sparked in 1978 when Workman Publishing released *Tomorrow and Beyond*. The book was edited by Random House art director Iain Summers and focused on a wide range of contemporary science-fiction artists. This was an uncommon approach at the time. It struck a chord with the young Arnie Fenner. Summers' book had no sequel, but Fenner couldn't help thinking, "What if there could be a book that highlighted the best contemporary artists in the fantasy, science-fiction and horror genres on a yearly basis?"

Fenner first floated the idea for the book to sci-fi artist Michael Whelan at Fool Con in 1980. During the early Eighties, Fenner would continue to brainstorm ideas with Whelan and others to figure out how to make a "Fantastic Art" (as Fenner coined the term) annual work. At the time, it was not a genre that was ready to be embraced by the public. The rather small community was relegated to a group of hard-core fans and industry people who would connect at the occasional modestly sized event.

Another source of early inspiration for Fenner came from the *Illustrators* annuals issued by New York's Society of Illustrators. This yearly collection had been showcasing prestigious artists in the editorial, advertising and other illustration fields since 1956, yet they included just a smattering of fantastic art back in the Seventies and Eighties. This was understandable, since fantasy and science fiction comprised a small portion of what was published each year. While the *Illustrators* annuals still hold incredible prestige to this day, Fenner

felt that the fantastic-art genre might have a shot on its own. Even with the success of *Star Wars*, it was a long-held belief among the public that such genre work was "just for kids" and therefore marginalized and ignored.

The "Science Fiction" group exhibition co-curated by Michael Whelan and Wayne D. Barlowe in 1984 at the Society of Illustrators' Museum of American Illustration provided further encouragement that a publication highlighting this genre might be possible. While initially intended to be a science-fiction show, fantasy and horror were introduced to the mix. Fenner recalled, "Everyone loved it: Illustrators both in and out of genre, educators, students, collectors, fans and casual visitors were all enthused. The exhibit created a huge buzz in the field. There had never been such an expansive gathering of fantasy and science-fiction artists in one place at one time before."

By the early Nineties, Cathy Fenner had joined her husband as a co-conspirator. They recognized that there was no singular book on the genre, and they saw the opportunity to create a community that could be nurtured. With the encouragement of Whelan—and with a healthy respect and admiration for the other organizations that came before, tied in with a love of the field—the Fenners had every bit of motivation to make their dream a reality.

After shopping their idea to publishers for a frustrating number of years, the Fenners finally reached the tipping point during a lunch in the early Nineties. "Let's stop talking about it and do it ourselves," declared Cathy. Though it was a frightening idea, they rallied together and agreed to push forward on their own. Arnie had been doing

Left: The *Spectrum* 25 awards backstage prior to the ceremony. The awards were made by J. Anthony Kosar and Kosart Studios. Right: John Fleskes with Flesk office manager Katherine Chu during the awards ceremony. Photos by Mark Berry.

The *Spectrum 25* awards ceremony was held on May 5, 2018, at the Brookledge Theater in Los Angeles. Clockwise from top left: Kristine and Colin Poole announce Miranda Meeks as the recipient of the Rising Star Award. The award-winners, from top left to right, include Tim O'Brien, Laurel Blechman, Victo Ngai, Miranda Meeks and Andrew Hem. The bottom row, from left to right, includes Michael MacRae, Edward Kinsella III, Anthony Francisco and Wangjie Li. Continuing on: William Stout takes part in the magic act during the show; group picture of the artists and guests; Victo Ngai onstage after receiving her gold award; and a group picture during the after-party. Photos by Mark Berry.

some design work for publisher Tim Underwood at the time. Once Underwood caught wind of what the Fenners were up to, he agreed to sign on as publisher. Underwood's involvement greatly increased its chances of success. The artist Rick Berry came up with the title *Spectrum*. Then Berry, Dave Stevens, Tim Kirk and Don Ivan Punchatz provided art for the inaugural "Call for Entries" poster. In 1994, the first juried *Spectrum* annual was released through worldwide distribution. *Spectrum* could be found at the major bookstore chains, in independent stores and in comics shops. It immediately became *the* book to get on the genre.

A Spectrum Advisory Board was assembled to offer suggestions and insight into an ever-changing marketplace as well as to vote upon the Grand Master each year. As the board members have rotated over the years, Brom is the only one to have remained for all twenty-five years. (As an aside, Brom and Scott Gustafson are the only two artists to be included in every volume of *Spectrum*.)

Spectrum has served as a time capsule to capture key moments in the fantastic-art world and to honor artistic achievements while also collecting the best works completed during the year. It also has traveled through the sudden changes in printing, as photographic plates were retired for the digital process, and welcomed the digital art that burst onto the scene. While some saw digital art as a threat to traditional art, time embraced both media. The delivery of art by use of photography and transparencies also came to an end, as scans and digital-file deliveries are now the standard.

The internet has provided opportunities for any artist to be seen, regardless of where he or she lives and what connections they have, and it evened the playing field so that a range of diversity can be seen today unlike at any other time. Artists have a reach into modern film and television that could not have been imagined in 1994. The brick-and-mortar stores took a devastating blow with many chains and independents now out of business. However, crowd-funding platforms combined with self-publishing are making more books available now than could ever be possible before. Book agents and publishers now compete with self-publishing while settling into a quickly changing marketplace that faces the challenges of far lower print runs than were seen in the Nineties.

With *Spectrum* 2 in 1995 came the first Grand Master award to recognize an icon in the field who had inspired generations. Frank Frazetta was the clear and obvious artist to set the benchmark for this award.

To further bring the community together, the Fenners envisioned an event that would focus entirely on the artists. Bob Self, publisher of Baby Tattoo Books, came up with the "Spectrum Fantastic Art Live" (SFAL) name. The event initially was planned for 2008, but the recession postponed it until the economy was more stabilized. Finally launched in 2012, SFAL coincided with the first *Spectrum* awards ceremony. The Fenners had long dreamed of an event where the artists could be spotlighted on a stage in an actual theater. The *Spectrum* 19 award nominees and recipients were recognized at the Midland Theater in Kansas City, Missouri, on May 19, 2012. The ceremony has been a yearly tradition ever since.

In 2013, we announced that *Spectrum* 20 would be the Fenners' last as editors and that I would step into the role of both editor and publisher. With *Spectrum* 21 we moved operations to our Flesk offices in Santa Cruz, California, and opened a new online-submissions process. For the *Spectrum* 22 awards ceremony—held on May 23, 2015, at the Folly Theater in Kansas City, Missouri—we introduced the completely new bronze "Muse" award, designed and sculpted by Colin and Kristine Poole. At that same time, the new "Rising Star" award was introduced to recognize an emerging artist. This award also was conceived by the Pooles, who select the recipient as well. Wylie Beckert was the first to be recognized as a Spectrum Rising Star. For the *Spectrum* 24 awards ceremony, J. Anthony Kosar was selected to reveal a new award that has carried us through to today.

We were thrilled to highlight the artists during a ceremony on May 5, 2018, held at the historic Brookledge Theater in Los Angeles. Both exclusive *and* intimate, the Brookledge is a unique venue operated by the owners of The Magic Castle, LA's legendary private club for professional magicians. The evening consisted of the presentations of the gold and silver awards for exemplary art in eight categories. Additionally, the Spectrum Grand Master and Rising Star award recipients where announced. Presenters included such luminaries of the art community as Alina Chau, Craig Elliott, Te Hu, Tim O'Brien, Iain McCaig, Brynn Metheney, Karla Ortiz, Colin and Kristine Poole, William Stout and Paul Sullivan. *Spectrum* co-founder Arnie Fenner introduced a memorial video devoted to the creatives who had passed away in the previous year. Bob Self served as the master of ceremonies during the evening, while I presented the final thank-you speech to cap off a special evening. We would like to thank Erika Larsen for granting us special permission to hold the ceremony at the Brookledge.

And, like the Fenners, I have many big ideas and plans that will be revealed and implemented in the future. For now, we get to celebrate the artists who fill the pages of *Spectrum* 25. They represent many of the best talents working in the fantastic arts today. In each annual, we highlight the artists, industry news and projects that made an impact during the past year by offering insight into eight categories. Thank you to everyone who submitted!

ADVERTISING

Artwork in this category was completed for advertising purposes and used in brochures, billboards, magazines, newspapers, posters for film, TV, packaging for videogames or music products, displays at events or in any other form that is used to promote an artist, event or item. Greg Ruth's "Moonrise," completed for The Criterion Collection's new release of the 1948 film *Moonrise*, received the gold award in the Advertising category. Laurel Blechman received the silver award for her painting "ComicBase 2018," which was created for the comic-book collection tracking program of the same name. The nominations for outstanding achievement go to "The Night Mare," by Brom; "Mixc World Launch," by Victo Ngai; and "SK-II Art of Travel packaging project: China," by Yuko Shimizu.

Other noteworthy contributions to the world of advertising included Donato Giancola's "St. George and the White Dragon," completed for GenCon's 50th anniversary, and Tim O'Brien's commission by the Cincinnati Opera to paint a portrait of Violetta for its La Traviata poster. Anna Dittmann created the EP art for "I Dreamt I Could Fly" for BlauDisS & Notion Waves. Alessandra Pisano continued working with Cu Dubh, this time creating her paintings "Revelations" and "Rhiannon" for the band's promotional efforts. Scott Gustafson, along with Frank Cho and Nathanna Erica, created posters for the *Animal Crackers* animated film. Kirbi Fagan illustrated a new personal work for Reckless Deck titled "Blind Circus." Victo Ngai, one of the preeminent artists working today, completed a slew of advertising work for Hong Kong Airlines, Johnnie Walker Blue Label Scotch and Prophecy Wines. And Yuko Shimizu was commissioned by SK-II to create six different packaging designs that are only available in duty-free stores at six different airports across Asia.

BOOK

This category includes works that were created for the cover or interior pages of a book. Victo Ngai received the gold award for her art for Christopher Caldwell's short novel "Serving Fish," published in *Fantastic Stories of the Imagination*. The jury recognized Petar Meseldzija's "The Old Man and the Forest" for the silver award.

Nominations highlight "Red Rising," by Tommy Arnold; "A Girl & Her Friends," by Wesley Burt; and "Heading Home, Spread 118," by Gregory Manchess.

As the sales for eBooks fell 10 percent when compared with 2016, overall tangible book sales saw an increase of 1.9 percent. However, bookstore sales fell 3.6 percent due to a sluggish five-month period ending with a very soft December. (Sales figures were gleaned from *Publisher's Weekly* year-end reports and the PGW State of the State report.) The best-selling new book of the year was the latest installment in Jeff Kinney's Wimpy Kid series, *The Getaway*. This is worth celebrating due to it being an illustrated book that is supported by younger readers with an appetite for print. As an aside, it's edited by Spectrum Advisory Board member Charlie Kochman.

One topic to note is the unknown quantity of direct sales generated by publishers and self-publishers who do not use distributors. With the option of self-publishing through crowd-funding platforms—as well as the marketing that can be done through personal social-media websites and at events—we continue to see a shift in the way artists reach their fan base. Books that are not viable for a publisher now can be packaged into a short run and sold directly by the artist.

The *Publisher's Weekly* Industry Salary Survey for 2017 showed a slight narrowing of the pay gap between men and women. One detail to note is that, out of all positions combined, the medium salary was $93,000 for men and $65,000 for women. This is despite women accounting for 80 percent of those positions. It is only in management where men hold the majority of positions, at 51 percent. (The full report can be read online at *publishersweekly.com*.)

Individual Art Collections

There was no shortage of premium art books in 2017. Our list is far from complete but highlights some noteworthy titles. Among them are *Classic Storybook Fables: Including "Beauty and the Beast" and Other Favorites* (Artisan), by Scott Gustafson; *The Movie Art of Syd Mead: Visual Futurist* (Titan Books); *Innsmouth: The Lost Drawings of Mannish Sycovia* (Alaxis Press), by Mark A. Nelson; *Never Lasting Miracles: The Art of Todd Schorr* (Last Gasp), a career retrospective with 87 new pieces; *Eliza Ivanova: Raw Material v.1*, a highlight for the year along with *Nocturnals: Sinister Path*, by Dan Brereton (both from Steven Morger); *The Sci-Fi & Fantasy Art of Patrick J. Jones* (Korero Press); *Sketching From Imagination: Characters* (3dtotal Publishing), packed with sketches by fifty different artists; *The Art of Posuka Demizu* (PIE International); *OTOMO: A Global Tribute to the Mind Behind Akira* (Kodansha Comics), which pays tribute to Katsuhiro Otomo with content by more than eighty fine artists; *Harry Potter: A Cinematic Gallery: 80 Original Images To Color and Inspire* (Insight Editions), with art by J.M. Dragunas; and *The Silver Way: Techniques, Tips and Tutorials for Effective Character Design* (Design Studio Press), by Stephen Silver, which "offers invaluable instruction from one of the best teachers in the industry."

Also on our list are *How Comics Work* (Wellfleet Press), by Dave Gibbons; *Norse Myths: Tales of Odin, Thor and Loki* (Candlewick Studio and Walker Studio), illustrated on nearly all of its 240 pages by Jeffrey Alan Love; *Goblin Market* (Donald M. Grant), which features over one hundred drawings and watercolors by Omar Rayyan; *Beginner's Guide to Sculpting Characters in Clay* (3dtotal Publishing), a self-explanatory title; *Sideshow Collectibles Presents: Capturing Archetypes, Volume 3: Astonishing Avengers, Adversaries, and Antiheroes* (Insight Editions), which gathers the latest from Sideshow Collectibles in a beautifully presented premium hardcover; *Above the Timberline* (Saga Press), by Gregory Manchess, lavishly illustrated with over 120 paintings; and *Timeless: Diego and the Rangers of the Vastlantic* (Katherine Tegen Books), packed with over 150 illustrations by Armand Baltazar.

Film, Animation and Gaming

The "Art of…" movie books provide rare insight into the years of work that go into producing a new feature film. Noteworthy titles include *The Art of Coco* (Chronicle Books), *Justice League: The Art of the Film* and *Wonder Woman: The Art and Making of the Film* (both from Titan Books). *Marvel's Guardians of the Galaxy Vol. 2: The Art of the Movie*, *Marvel's Thor: Ragnarok: The Art of the Movie* and *Spider-Man: Homecoming: The Art of the Movie* (all from Marvel) include concept art by the visual-development teams. Guillermo del Toro's *The Shape of Water: Creating a Fairy Tale for Troubled Times* explores the art and making of the Oscar-winning film, while *The Art of Mondo* brings together classic film-art posters (both from Insight Editions). Also notable are *The Art of Star Wars: The Last Jedi* (Harry N. Abrams) and *The Art of Star Trek: The Kelvin Timeline* and *Star Trek Beyond: The Makeup Artistry of Joel Harlow* (both from Titan Books). Gaming is a dominant part of the industry that attracts some of its brightest stars, and the following books provide a glimpse into the work being done to bring these games to life: *The Art of Assassin's Creed Origins* and *The Art of Horizon Zero Dawn* (Titan Books); *The Art of Destiny, Volume 2* (Insight Editions); *Project 77* (ArtStation Media); and *Blizzard Entertainment's The Art of Overwatch* and *Overwatch: Anthology Volume 1* (Dark Horse Books).

COMICS

The Comics category highlights covers, splashes or pages used in comic books, graphic novels, newspaper strips, online features and any other sequential-art storytelling devices. Alex Alice's Castle in the Stars Book 2, pages 60-61, a two-page sequential spread, took the gold award. Gary Gianni received the silver award for *Hellboy: Into the Silent Sea*, page 11, which was first published by Dark Horse and then in an oversized deluxe format by Flesk. The highlighted nominations include *Kratos*, by E.M. Gist; *Shirtless Bear Fighter #4* variant cover, by Paolo Rivera; and *Ugly Cinderwench and the Very Angry Ghost*, page 3, by Xaviere Daumarie.

The big news in 2017 was that diversity is working. We're all benefitting by it through great stories and art by fresh voices. There are two lists of top-ten graphic novels of 2017 available that highlight this change. The first list is shared by Diamond Comic Distributors. Diamond markets primarily to the independent comic-book stores. The second list is compiled by Bookscan, which tracks sales through the national book trade. This includes the library market and independent bookstores as examples. If you analyze the two lists, you will see a variation in the order and the titles listed, but you also will see that women, Asians and African-Americans have a strong representation in the creative teams and in the characters in leading roles. You will also note that only one superhero title is included on both lists.

After a big push by the public throughout previous years for greater diversity in comics, we're seeing that non-superhero titles are setting the tone and being rewarded for it. At the top of the Diamond list of best-selling graphic novels we have *Saga* (Image), with art by Fiona Staples, taking the first two spots. It's followed by *The Walking Dead* (Image), with art by Charlie Adlard; *Paper Girls* (Image), with art by Cliff Chiang; *Batman Vol. 1: I Am Gotham* (DC), with art by David Finch; and *Monstress* (Image), with art by Sana Takeda, taking the sixth spot. The Bookscan adult graphic-novel list includes *March: Book One* (Top Shelf Productions) in first place with the *March* trilogy set at number four. *March* is drawn by Nate Powell and features the memoir of Georgia Rep. John Lewis. *Saga* is at number two, followed by *Everyone's a Aliebn When Ur a Aliebn Too* (HarperCollins), by Jomney Sun, followed by *The Walking Dead* in the fifth spot.

Marvel's position as the top comic publisher of the year has, with no doubt, been supported by the popularity of its Marvel Studios films. Previously obscure characters outside of the comics world, such

Eliza Ivanova: Raw Material v. 1 is an astonishing new book of drawings she has done over the last five years.

Hellboy: Krampusnacht (Dark Horse Comics) is Mike Mignola's story that pitted Hellboy against a satanic spin on Santa that was gorgeously drawn by Adam Hughes. Artwork shown is page 1 of the story.

as Black Panther, are becoming household names. Marvel utilized its top artists for covers, including Mark Brooks and J. Scott Campbell on *Secret Empire*. Alex Ross continues as one of the preeminent cover artists in the industry over the last twenty years with his cover for *Avengers* #9. Exceptional interior artists include Paul Renaud on *Captain America: Sam Wilson* #20, Russell Dauterman on *The Mighty Thor*, Stuart Immonen on *Amazing Spider-Man* #29, Sara Pichelli on *Spider-Man*, Greg Smallwood on *Moon Knight*, Leinil Francis Yu on *Secret Empire* #6 and Christian Ward on *Black Bolt*. The publisher's top seller for 2017 was *Marvel Legacy* #1, featuring a variant cover by Terry Dodson and interior art by Chris Samnee and others. Another popular title was *Phoenix Resurrection: The Return of Jean Grey*, with art by Leinil Francis Yu.

Ranked as the No. 2 comic publisher of the year, DC Comics' best-selling title was *Dark Knights: Metal* #1, with art by Greg Capullo. *Doomsday Clock* #2, with art by Gary Frank, is included in the top-ten list for the year. Frank Cho continued his highly popular variant-edition covers for the *Harley Quinn* series. Cho showed his playful side by injecting illicit humor into the themes running throughout the year, which brought forth comparisons—and fans—from his *Liberty Meadows* comic-strip days. *The Art of Harley Quinn* is packed with iconic comic covers and panels outlining the history of this wildly popular character. Also notable was the new limited series *Batman: White Knight*, written and drawn by Sean Murphy. *Super Sons* #1 arrived early in the year, with art by the rising new talent Jorge Jimenez. Nick Derington tackled *Doom Patrol* with exceptional results. DC's other outstanding comics included *Mister Miracle*, with art by Mitch Gerards; *Batman*, with art by Jöelle Jones; *Aquaman*, with art by Stjepan Sejic; and *Shade the Changing Girl*, with art by Marley Zarcone. While not a comic book, *Wonder Woman*—the seventh highest-grossing film of 2017, boasting a female star and director— was an influential movie that will undoubtedly help to introduce more diversity into the field.

Dark Horse released *Hellboy: Into the Silent Sea*, drawn by Gary Gianni, whose working methods and style harken back to the great masters of a bygone era. Gianni spent a full year conducting research, photographing models and drawing thumbnails—all of which gave him the proper foundation to draw exquisitely rendered comic pages. *Hellboy in Hell Library Edition* is an oversized collection of the series that includes a bonus sketchbook section. Geof Darrow properly twisted the minds of young people with *Shaolin Cowboy: Who'll Stop the Reign?* And *Lead Poisoning: The Art of Geof Darrow* captured more bizarre work from Darrow. Richard and Wendy Pini continued *Elfquest: Final Quest* as the series neared its final issue after forty years of pointed ears. *Hellboy: Krampusnacht*, with art by Adam Hughes, was among the best-drawn comics of the year. And Neil Gaiman's *American Gods: Shadows* #1 was a top seller for Dark Horse while featuring art by Scott Hampton.

Image continues its dominance as a publisher of independent creator-owned comics. Andrew Maclean furthered his captivating and fun *Head Lopper* comic series with the *Crimson Tower* storyline. Cliff Chiang is creating a true legacy for himself with *Paper Girls*. He's an exceptional artist who can draw anything while having a strong ability to pace and tell a story. Fiona Staples set the stage in 2012 with *Saga* as one of the best-selling comics in the industry. Sana Takeda can be mentioned among the top comic artists today for her work on *Monstress*. *Tokyo Ghost Complete Edition*, by Sean Murphy, is packed with extra designs, sketches and bonus material. Other artists published by Image who are worth discovering for yourself are Daniel Warren Johnson on *Extremity*, Dustin Nguyen on *Descender*, Jerome Opeña on *Seven to Eternity*, Sean Phillips on *Kill or Be Killed*, Matteo Scalera on *Dead Body Road*, Hayden Sherman on *The Few*, Babs Tarr on *Motor Crush* and Skottie Young on *I Hate Fairyland*.

Additional noteworthy releases in 2017 included *The Unsound*, with art by Jack T. Cole, and the conclusion of *Skybourne* by Frank Cho (both from Boom! Studios). *My Favorite Thing Is Monsters* (Fantagraphics) became everyone's favorite graphic novel for the year with Emil Ferris' intricate drawings and her captivating narrative. Also outstanding were *Nightlights* (Nobrow Press), by Lorena Alvarez, and *The Dam Keeper* (First Second), by Robert Kondo and Dice Tsutsumi.

CONCEPT ART

The Concept Art category includes pieces made primarily for films and videogames, but they also are imperative in areas such as theater and television. These rarely seen works are used to visually convey ideas to directors, producers and anyone else directly involved. Often unknown to the general public, their creators play a crucial role in defining the look and feel of the biggest games and blockbuster movies that are enjoyed by millions of people worldwide. Out of the ten top-grossing films in 2017, six were superhero-related. Fantasy, horror and animated genres are also on the list. *Star Wars: The Last Jedi* was the No. 1 film. The top-grossing videogame of the year was *Call of Duty: WWII*, with *Destiny 2* coming in second. All of these films and videogames relied heavily on concept artists to provide character, creature, vehicle, item and object props as well as environment/background designs to make them successful and enjoyable.

The Concept Art gold award went to Wangjie Li for his work titled "Battlefield Scene." The silver award was bestowed on Anthony Francisco, the senior visual development concept illustrator at Marvel Studios, for his "Okoye and Nakia the Dora Milaje" piece. This design has been wildly popular since the release of the Black Panther film. The nominations include "Transformers 5 Autobot Design 'Canopy,'" by Wesley Burt; "Ganesh Gangis," by Te Hu; and "Geisha Interior (Ghost in the Shell)," by Nick Keller.

There's no shortage of "Art of…" books that highlight work done for these films and videogame properties. However, much of the concept art completed over the course of the year is not included in these books due to confidentiality agreements. There are, however, many artists with superior abilities who have stood out over the year. A short list includes the following people. Sung Choi does exceptional work for Bungie's *Destiny* videogame and also creates art for Wizards of the Coast and Blizzard Entertainment. Dylan Cole, the artist behind the thirty different teaser movie posters for *Star Wars: The Force Awakens*, is currently the co-production designer for the *Avatar* sequels. Ian McQue, a consummate doodler, is an outstanding master of the line whose drawings of people, robots, buildings, weaponry and vehicles will astound you. The *Halo* art director Sparth, who also creates the book series *Structura* (Design Studio Press), is a master of color and environments. Wesley Burt, whose concept art is actively utilized for the Marvel cinematic universe, should also be recognized for his work on all five *Transformers* films. And Iain McCaig and Karla Ortiz manage to find time to serve as advisers on *Spectrum* while also defining the looks of the most iconic characters seen on screens today.

DIMENSIONAL

Sculptures created for model kits, collectibles and editorial or fine art comprise the dimensional category. The Dimensional gold award goes to Forest Rogers for her evocative "Octopoid Descending" sculpture. The silver award recognizes the work of Jessica Dalva for her piece titled "I'll Need Entire Cities To Replace You." The nominations for achievement go to "Life and Death," by Patrick Masson; "Cthulhu 22 Inch Tall Statue," by DopePope; and "Statue of Piece," by Akihito.

Sideshow Collectibles continued to surprise and impress in 2017 with the unveiling of one of its most-anticipated maquettes, "Thanos on

"Talula and the Stray," by the Shiflett brothers. It is the story of a little girl and a dragon, but which is "Talula" and which "the Stray"? The Shifletts keep that part intentionally ambiguous as people ask who had rescued whom? It was originally sculpted in Super Sculpey Firm. It has been produced in both resin and bronze. The sculpture stands 12 inches tall, with a 13.5-inch wingspan.

Throne." Created with the help of thirteen artists and two Sideshow teams, this statue pushes the boundaries with its quality, size and intricate details.

Brian Kesinger—one of the leading artists in the world of Steampunk, the creator of *Traveling With Your Octopus* and the popular mash-up of *Star Wars* and *Calvin & Hobbes*—has contributed to the world of sculpture with his delightful "Aagar the Emotional." Dan Chudzinski, who works as the curator at the Mazza Museum in Findlay, Ohio, continues to share his talent by creating new and unique creature pieces that bring the imagination to life. A three-time *Spectrum* nominee, Dug Stanat never fails to amaze with his eerie and monstrous creations. J. Anthony Kosar, the founder of Kosart Studios and creator of the *Spectrum* 24 and 25 awards, scares and delights with his realistic creatures, characters and excellent FX work. And the Shiflett brothers, *Spectrum* 21 gold award-winners, create iconic works and remarkable originals that are hard to miss and never cease to amaze.

EDITORIAL

The Editorial category includes art appearing mainly in magazines or newspapers. This year's gold award went to Edward Kinsella III's "My Whereabouts," which was done for *Playboy*. Kinsella's yearning for an unmistakable voice has led to a refined style that is capturing the attention of the public and his peers. Tim O'Brien's "Nothing To See Here" was the silver award recipient. It was used for the February 27, 2017, cover of *Time*. O'Brien has been featured over a dozen times on the magazine's cover. The nominees include works by three superlative artists who proved how difficult it is for the judges to make

their final decisions: "The Rise," by Yoann Lossel; "SK-II Art of Travel packaging project: Japan," by Yuko Shimizu; and "Sports Stopwatch," by Victo Ngai.

Airbrush Action featured a cover by Galen Dara on its July-August issue, along with a feature on the *Spectrum* 24 award recipients. *Amazing Figure Modeler* continued its focus on comprehensive modeling instructions by some of the best modelers in the business. 3dtotal Publishing launched its new magazine *CDQ: Character Design Quarterly*, aimed toward providing tips and techniques to students and professionals. *GRAPHITE 3: Concept Drawing, Illustration, Urban Sketching*, another new publication by 3dtotal, features interviews and tutorials on drawing and sketching. The science-fiction and fantasy magazine *Clarksworld* utilized artists such as Julie Dillon, Matt Dixon and Eddie Mendoza to illustrate its covers each month. *Beautiful Bizarre*, a quarterly print and digital art magazine, features artists from the fantastic-art genre. Highlights include articles on Camilla d'Errico, Tran Nguyen and Aron Wiesenfeld. And *ImagineFX* is essential for its monthly tutorials, galleries, interviews and highlights that will keep you apprised and inspired.

INSTITUTIONAL

The Institutional category includes professional works not obviously covered in the other categories. As such, art found within this section covers a wide gamut of the industry, most notably for role-playing games and card art and including pieces for announcements, annual reports, calendars, greeting cards, prints, portfolios, posters, collectibles and website graphics. You will find an eclectic gathering of material that spans a considerable breath within the industry. Seb

Left: Cover for *Timeless: Diego and the Rangers of the Vastlantic* (Katherine Tegen Books), which integrates text and art with over 150 illustrations by Armand Baltazar. Right: As a follow-up to her first art book, *Blush*, *Coral: The Art of Pernille Ørum* collects Ørum's favorite off-the-clock artwork created from 2015 to 2017 in one beautifully made book. Ørum is a lead character designer on DC Superhero Girls who regularly finds time to focus on personal projects.

McKinnon's "Stasis" was the recipient of the gold award, while Piotr Jabłonski's "Moaning Wall" received the silver award. Both pieces were done for Magic: The Gathering, with Dawn Murin and Cynthia Sheppard serving as art directors. The nominations include "Three Color Trilogy Blue," by Victo Ngai; "Dinosaur Hunter," by Tianhua X; and "Vraska," by Chris Rahn.

Wizards of the Coast, a titan in the industry, announced its new game *Magic: The Gathering Arena*, a digital version similar to their classic card game and currently in beta mode, which will open new doors to gameplay in today's digital world. Blizzard had a record number of attendees at its BlizzCon event and made several big announcements, including a new *Overwatch* hero named Moira, a map called "Blizzardworld," a *Hearthstone* expansion titled "Kobolds & Catacombs" and a new free version of *StarCraft 2: Wings of Liberty*.

Sylvia Ritter, a new and upcoming artist, enchants with her vibrant style and unique use of color. Lucas Graciano, who already has several awards under his belt, continues to demonstrate his dynamic style in epic works of art. Sean Andrew Murray, creator of the city of *Gateway* and a well-known concept artist and illustrator, showcased his skills through his stunning details and elaborate art pieces. Vanessa Lemen's evocative and passionate style brings a new element to this industry, and the intensity of her emotions can be seen in her work. Though known for her comic-book covers for all major publishers, Tula Lotay crosses industries with her expressive style and eloquent work.

Outstanding calendars released for the 2018 season include *Boris Vallejo and Julie Bell's Fantasy Wall Calendar 2018* (Workman Publishing); *Women of Myth & Magic 2018 Fantasy Art Wall Calendar* (Amber Lotus Publishing), by Kinuko Y. Craft; *Llewellyn's 2018 Shadowscapes Calendar* (Llewellyn Publications), by Stephanie Pui-Mun Law; *Tolkien Calendar 2018* (HarperCollins), by Alan Lee; and *George R. R. Martin: A Song of Ice and Fire 2018 Calendar* (Bantam), illustrated by Eric Velhagen.

UNPUBLISHED

The Unpublished category features art completed for galleries, speculative assignments or ongoing projects to be published in the future. Student work is also welcomed here, along with experimental studies. What makes this section special is that it affords anyone, regardless of stature or position, the opportunity to be a part of *Spectrum*. Found here are emerging artists who may be showing their works for the first time, along with artists who are at the top of their game with decade's worth of paintings and drawings that continue to feed legions of fans. All stand here as equals.

Andrew Hem took the top honor with his gold award for "Whirlpool." Michael MacRae wowed the judges to secure the silver ward for his "Tip of the Spear." The nominations include "Star Wars Triptych," by Iain McCaig; "Dim Stars," by Scott Bakal; and "Ella Standing Between Earth and Sky," by Howard Lyon.

Exhibitions/Events/Signings

Gallery art for solo and group exhibitions also is well-represented here. Some of the best pieces being produced today are those personal works done purely based on the artists' desire to paint what they want to paint. The results are often exhilarating. Galleries and art shows are excellent resources for viewing or purchasing original

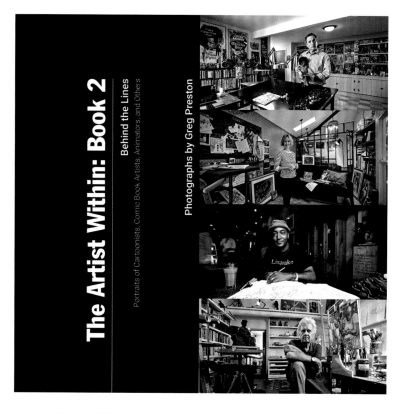

Left: *The Artist Within: Book 2* is the culmination of almost thirty years of photography by Greg Preston. This book is a living history of the men and women who have shaped the field. Right: Mike Azevedo's "Grook Fu Master" card art from *Mean Streets of Gadgetzan*, the fourth expansion to *Hearthstone: Heroes of Warcraft*, released by Blizzard Entertainment. This final art is reproduced here after an unfinished version was printed in *Spectrum 24*.

works that directly benefit the living artists. Many galleries feature exclusive solo and group exhibitions at art events, making these shows worthwhile to visit. While there are far more than can be noted here, a selection of exhibits include the following.

Into the Unknown: A Journey Through Science Fiction, curated by Patrick Gyger and Barbican International Enterprises, opened at the Barbican Centre in London on June 3, 2017, to rave reviews. More than 800 works were on display. The show traveled to Athens, Greece, where it opened on October 10 at the Onassis Cultural Centre.

The Haven Gallery in New York City put on a number of solo and group exhibits that featured artists found within the pages of *Spectrum* and throughout related genres. Highlights included Annie Stegg Gerard's "Halcyon Garden," which opened on June 24. "Halcyon Garden is an exploration of the small hidden worlds that exist in our own backyards and the drama that unfolds between their unseen inhabitants," shares Gerard. "The show was composed of twelve paintings of narrative and evocative imagery that illustrate the mystery in a hidden moment of time and the veiled secrets that are waiting to be discovered." Gerard, Kukula, Travis Louie, Dan Quintana and a number of other artists represented by Haven exhibited at the Market Art + Design show at the Bridgehampton Museum on July 6-9. Original works by Camilla d'Errico, Forest Rogers, Virginie Ropars, Erika Sanada and a few dozen others were shown at the Heart's Blood group show, which opened at Haven on September 16 and was curated by *Beautiful Bizarre Magazine*. The opening reception of "Stephanie Law: Where the Sea Meets the Sky" on December 2 featured fourteen new paintings of Law's mythological worlds. Haven revealed five new paintings depicting Eastern female deities by Chie Yoshii and five watercolors by Omar Rayyan at its booth during the

Scope art show in Miami in early December. Allessandra Pisano's painting "Rhiannon," inspired by the Fleetwood Mac song of the same name, was completed for Haven's Music Box III group show, which ran from January 13 to February 18. Pieces by Adam S. Doyle and Sam Guay were also included.

Jessica Dalva's exhibition "Mess" opened on November 3 at the La Luz de Jesus Gallery in Los Angeles. Over a dozen new sculptures, drawings and paintings were revealed. The creation of these fascinating works is described by Dalva: "This series of sculptures, drawings and paintings were, in great part, brought about as a response to the many disconcerting and unbelievable circumstances that have become commonplace recently. It has been difficult to create artwork in the midst of unprecedented disquiet, so these pieces were attempts to use the frustration and uncertainty we have been facing as a form of small resistance and personal countermeasure." The premiere and signing of J.A.W. Cooper's three books *Familiars*, *Flora & Fauna* and *Viscera* was held at the gallery on November 4.

The Museum of the Shenandoah Valley was the first to host the traveling exhibition *Superheroes and Superstars: The Works of Alex Ross*. Nearly one hundred works were on view beginning on February 11. This event was initially shown at the Norman Rockwell Museum, where it was organized. The curator is Jesse Kowalski.

A *Spectrum* 24 book-signing event was held on November 18 at the CTN Animation Expo in Burbank, California.

Gallery Nucleus in Alhambra is the premier site in Southern California for book launches and exhibits, and it serves as welcome gathering place for the community. A select sample of events held there in 2017 includes a solo exhibition of the work of Nico Delort on February 11. Delort is a unique artist admired for his intricate scratchboard pieces. Blizzard Entertainment was highlighted with an

Cover painting for *Above the Timberline* (Saga Press), by Gregory Manchess. The book is lavishly illustrated with over 120 paintings. It tells the story of the son of a famed explorer searching for his stranded father and a lost city buried under the snows of a future frozen Earth. The Society of Illustrators in New York City presented a selection of works from this highly anticipated book. The opening reception was held on September 28, 2017.

art exhibition and book launch for *The Art of Overwatch* that began on October 14. Eliza Ivanova had her first solo show with an opening reception on November 18. The show revealed dozens of her exquisite drawings and served as the premiere for her new book *Raw Material v.1*. And a *Spectrum* 24 celebration and book signing was held on December 16 with over a dozen of the artists featured in attendance.

Sketchpad Gallery in San Francisco is a terrific new venue run by a passionate and energetic crew. February 4 brought the concept artists Christian Alzmann, Erik Tiemens and Tyler Scarlet together for *The Art of Rogue One: A Star Wars Story* book signing. "Leading Ladies" opened on February 25 and showcased original art celebrating the iconic female leads of the films we love.

The self-explanatory "100 Artists, 100 Pieces, 100 Square Inches" group exhibition highlighted those in the editorial, concept art and fine-art fields and opened on March 11. Steven Russell Black, George Cwirko-Godycki, Brynn Metheney, Andrew Theophilopoulos and 96 others adorned the walls. A *Spectrum* 23 book signing was held on March 18 with over a dozen artists in attendance. And another dozen artists made an appearance for the *Spectrum* 24 book signing on December 2.

The Society of Illustrators in New York City presented a selection of works from Greg Manchess' highly anticipated and lavish book *Above the Timberline*. The opening reception was held on September 28.

Spoke Art in San Francisco welcomed Eliza Ivanova, Karla Ortiz, Nadezda and Ximena Rendon for their group show "Four Dames" on March 7. Tara McPherson made an appearance there at Spoke's one-

day pop-up show on November 5. Meanwhile, at Spoke's New York City location, J.A.W. Cooper opened her solo show "Impermanence" on August 5. New graphite drawings and paintings featured Cooper's technique of gradually layering washes of acrylic or gouache over India ink. And on September 29, over one hundred artists celebrated the Japanese animator Hayao Miyazaki with new pieces to adorn the New York gallery's walls.

As for workshops, *Spectrum* has a long history of supporting our friends at The Illustration Academy in Kansas City, Missouri. The cornerstone of the program is that student artists are learning from working professionals in the visual arts. Allowing students to work under the guidance of groundbreaking artists as their mentors opens up an amazing opportunity for aspiring artists of all ages. *Spectrum* award-winners Edward Kinslella III, Jeffrey Alan Love, Victo Ngai and Grand Master Bill Sienkiewicz, along with Jon Foster and George Pratt, are just a handful of the instructors.

Today we continue to build a community where everyone can feel welcome. We want our actions today to benefit our future leaders. Our goal is to make sure there is a positive environment for a new age of artists who will define the future in another twenty-five years from now. We look forward to producing the *Spectrum* 26 awards ceremony on March 30, 2019, at the Folly Theater in Kansas City, Missouri, where we will continue our mission statement to raise the awareness of the artists while keeping this community our core driving force.

John Fleskes

BERNIE WRIGHTSON, 1948-2017
by WILLIAM STOUT

A great, dark sorrow sank into 2017's horror, comics and fantasy communities with the passing of our friend, artist Bernie Wrightson.

Raised (appropriately) in Edgar Allan Poe's Baltimore, Wrightson first caught the public's attention with a bit of fan art published in the letters section in *Creepy* #9. Even back then, Bernie seemed to "get" things on every level, recognizing how to conjure the essence of what fans and aficionados loved. His kindred spirits in the comics-fan community celebrated fifty years ago when Wrightson trailblazed his way from fandom into the Big League of DC Comics.

Bernie will forever be remembered for his ten-issue DC run of *Swamp Thing* (a character he co-created with writer Len Wein) and the celebrated *Frankenstein* pen illustrations that brought him even greater acclaim (as well as patronage from some heavy-hitting art collectors). Bernie brought the Wrightson Touch to *Batman* and *Spider-Man* and eventually came full circle back to his never-forgotten fan roots with his dazzling work for the pages of *Creepy* and *Eerie*. His dramatic portrayals of dinosaurs further fired our imaginations, helping us to see them anew. During this time, Wrightson (who went by Berni back then) co-founded The Studio, an

East Coast phenomenon that included Michael Kaluta, Jeffrey Jones and Barry Windsor-Smith—a real inspiration to all of us envious Left Coasters. Following his stint on *Ghostbusters*, the monster master moved to Los Angeles and became the movie biz's go-to guy for creature design.

Wrightson's basic comics style could be described as Frank Frazetta's solid drawing and brushmanship combined with the truly disturbing visions of EC's Graham Ingels. Bernie's own brushwork helped inspire colleagues like Dave Stevens, Mark Schultz, Frank Cho and yours truly to keep the disappearing tradition of brush-inking alive.

As a man, Bernie was as gracious in person as his art was solid. He had friends everywhere, all connected with a shared love of monsters, dinosaurs and EC comics. We were all delighted when Bernie finally met the love of his life, Liz—a real sweetheart, as Al Williamson would have called her, and one of the best things that ever happened to our pal.

Those lucky enough to know Bernie have lost a dear, dear friend. But the world at large has lost a truly great artist. Though his mortal form has passed into the land beyond beyond, his magnificent body of work lives on forever.

Left: "Butterfly Knight," by James Christensen. Right: Original art of Bernie Wrightson's iconic cover for *Swamp Thing* #1, originally published in 1972. Scan courtesy of Heritage Auctions, *ha.com*. Artwork copyright © 2018 DC Comics. All rights reserved.

JAMES CHRISTENSEN, 1942-2017
by BILL CARMAN

James Christensen did the first in-class demonstration I'd ever seen. The secret had been laid out before me. Who needed all that talk of learning to draw and studying rules? I went home with a smile on my face and new energy. After folding a wet paper towel and placing it on a plate, I laid out the exact colors in the exact order using the same acrylics that Professor Christensen used. I touched the brush—identical to his, of course—to the gessoed panel and waited for the magic. After the first stroke, I could hear the audible fart sound in my head. Never finished that painting, as I recall. At a time before the internet, when information was hard to come by, I was fortunate to have James Christensen as a main conduit of information.

A journey through the world of art with James Christensen was magical. His demos in figure-drawing class, his preliminary sketches for illustrations and especially his sketchbooks showed me the value of learning to draw. He started me on my journey of painting, guided my path to lifelong learning and set the example for my future as a teacher.

As a student and every time I was able to see him later in life, I couldn't wait to hear Jim's greeting, "Hullo, Willard." I've hated every nickname, pet name or endearing name anyone has ever tried to give me—except that one. His demeanor put those around him at ease. I can't remember ever seeing him in a hurry. In the classroom, students wanted to listen, and everywhere he went people wanted to be around him. Part of it was Jim's brilliant work, but even more it was his genuine happiness.

Perhaps my favorite memories come from evenings spent in his home or up at his fantasy cabin with the slate roof, large sculpted fireplace, painted and carved hunchbacks and fairies, spiral staircases and requisite secret bookcase-doorway to his studio. Those evenings were filled with eating and laughing and game-playing. He introduced me to the world of guided games and space marines. Each time we played, Jim would bring a new array of painted fantasy characters, monsters or armored marines. I will never forget the huge grin that always accompanied his anticipation of our reactions to the revelation of new figurines. He collected and painted thousands of those little pewter and plastic characters and brought new ones every time we played. I remain convinced that part of the reason he did so was to bring a little joy to his students and friends.

James Christensen was a teacher, mentor and friend to me and left an indelible impression on a lot of lives. His work will endure because of its wit, magic and beauty, but he will be remembered for his happiness, love of family and his faith. I remember asking him about an incredible painting with dark subject matter and whether he might ever paint cool stuff like this. He praised the painting but then looked at me with that twinkle in his eye and said, "Dark is easy. Go for the light."

REQUIEM

In 2018 we sadly remember the passing of these valued members of our community:

Alan Aldridge [b 1943] Artist
Xavier Atencio [b 1919] Animator
Edmund Bagwell [b 1967] Comic Artist
Magdalena A. Bakanowicz [b 1930] Sculptor
Jill Barklem [b 1951] Artist
Leo Baxendale [b 1930] Cartoonist
Rebecca Bond [b 1972] Artist
Dick Bruna [b 1927] Artist
Rich Buckler [b 1949] Comic Artist
Tommy Castillo [b 1971] Comic Artist
James C. Christensen [b 1942] Artist
José Luis Cuevas [b 1934] Artist
Nathan David [b 1930] Sculptor
Eduardo del Rio [b 1934] Cartoonist
Jay E. Disbrow [b 1926] Comic Artist
Chiara Fumai [b 1978] Artist
Pascal Garray [b 1965] Cartoonist
Robert Givens [b 1918] Animator
Sam Glanzman [b 1924] Comic Artist
Paul Goble [b 1933] Artist

Basil Gogos [b 1939] Artist
Karl Otto Götz [b 1914] Artist
Mary Hamilton [b 1936] Artist
Joe Harris [b 1928] Animator
Hugh Hefner [b 1926] Cartoonist/Publisher
Barkley L. Hendricks [1945] Artist
Masatoyo Kishi [b 1924] Artist
Jan Kruis [b 1933] Comic Artist
Dick Locher [b 1929] Cartoonist
Bob Lubbers [b 1922] Cartoonist
Jay Lynch [b1945] Comix Artist
Arthur Mather [b 1925] Comic Artist
Jill McElmurry [b 1955] Artist
Gustav Metzger [b 1926] Artist
Kate Millett [b 1934] Artist/Activist
John Mollo [b 1931] Costume Designer
Angel Mora [b 1925] Cartoonist
Alan Peckolick [b 1940] Designer
Kim Poor [b 1952] Artist
Keith Robinson [b 1955] Cartoonist
Pierre Seron [b 1942] Comic Artist
Dan Spiegle [b 1920] Comic Artist
James Stevenson [b 1929] Cartoonist
Niro Taniguchi [b 1948] Manga Artist

Valton Tyler [b 1944] Artist
John Watkiss [b 1961] Artist
Skip Williamson [b 1944] Comix Artist
Bernie Wrightson [b 1948] Artist
Jack Ziegler [b 1942] Cartoonist
Gino D'Achille [b 1935] Artist
Francis Xavier Atencio [b 1919] Animator
Jim Baikie [b 1940] Comic Artist
Roger Garland [b 1950] Artist
Pascal Garray [b 1965] Comic Artist
Dick Gautier [b 1931] Actor/Artist
Brooke Goffstein [b 1940] Artist
Joe Harris [b 1928] Animator
Dave Hunt [b 1942] Comic Artist
Carolyn Kelly [b ?] Cartoonist
Victor Llamas [b 1976] Comic Artist
Arthur Mather [b 1925] Comic Artist
George McGinnis [b 1931] Designer
Jack Mendelsohn [b 1926] Artist
Kim Poor [b 1952] Artist
Lona Rietschel [b 1939] Comic Artist
Norio Shioyama [b 1940] Artist
Gallup Tekin [b 1958] Comic Artist

SPECTRUM 25

THE BEST IN CONTEMPORARY FANTASTIC ART

ADVERTISING GOLD AWARD

GREG RUTH
MOONRISE

Medium: Graphite on paper *Size:* 10 x 12 in. *Art Director:* Eric Skillman

"To me, the award is about the work and a celebration of the work we all do as a community."

Greg Ruth is an illustrator who has been creating books and comics since 1993 and has published works through *The New York Times*, Mondo, DC Comics, Fantagraphics Books, Dark Horse, HarperCollins, Macmillan, Hyperion, Simon & Schuster, Random House, Slate, CNN, Penguin, Blumhouse, Paramount Pictures, A24 and Tor. He is the author of *The New York Times* best-sellers *The Lost Boy* and (with Ethan Hawke) *Indeh*. He also created two music videos for Prince and Rob Thomas and has worked on nearly a dozen children's picture books, including *Our Enduring Spirit* (with Barack Obama), *Red Kite, Blue Kite* (with Ji Li Jiang), *Rolling Thunder* (with Kate Mesner) and *Old Turtle: Questions of the Heart* (with Douglas Wood). Ruth currently is working on the graphic novel *Meadowlark* (also with Ethan Hawke) and lives and works in Western Massachusetts.

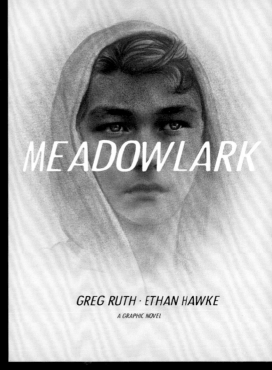

Photo by Alan Amato

Cover to *Meadowlark*, written by
Greg Ruth and Ethan Hawke

ADVERTISING SILVER AWARD

LAUREL BLECHMAN
COMICBASE 2018

Medium: Oil *Size:* 18 x 26.75 in. *Client:* Human Computing *Art Director:* Peter Bickford

"This award, coming from my peers at a time of great personal loss, means so much to me. It was totally unexpected and deeply appreciated. Besides providing a legitimate showcase for sci-fi and fantasy art when there was none, the great people at Spectrum have fostered a sense of community and inclusiveness that can't be underestimated. We all become better artists sharing our creativity!"

Laurel Blechman has been an award-winning illustrator and teacher for over thirty years. For twenty-eight years, she shared her life and studio with the late Glen Orbik—painting, teaching and accumulating more artwork, costumes, props and comics than one house can hold. As a student, she was mentored by the influential teacher Fred Fixler, as was Orbik, and she feels passionate about passing on Fixler's teaching legacy, mentoring and empowering new artists. Her partial client list includes DC Comics, Marvel Comics, Scholastic Books, Berkley Books, Hard Case Crime, Sony, 20th Century Fox and Penzoil. Blechman also has served as a board member of the Society of Illustrators of Los Angeles. She is in the process of compiling books on Glen Orbik's artwork.

Photo by Glen Orbik

Ghostrider poster *Client:* Marvel Comics

Brom

Title: The Night Mare *Medium:* Oil *Size:* 48 x 60 in. *Client:* IX Arts

Victo Ngai
Title: Mixc World Launch *Medium:* Mixed media *Size:* 65 x 23 ft. *Client:* Mixc World *Art Director:* Yong Liu

Yuko Shimizu
Title: SK-II Art of Travel packaging project: CHINA
Medium: Ink drawing with digital color   *Client:* NiCE Singapore, P&G Asia   *Art Director:* Fabian Serrano, Magdalena Gacek

Yuko Shimizu
Title: Takumi
Medium: Ink drawing with digital color
Client: Asatsu DK, Mitsui PR Committee

Yuko Shimizu
Title: SK-II Art of Travel
packaging project: JAPAN
Medium: Ink drawing with digital color
Client: NiCE Singapore and P&G Asia
Art Director: Fabian Serrano
and Magdalena Gacekv

Tim O'Brien
Title: La Traviata *Medium:* Oil on board
Size: 15 x 19 in. *Client:* Cincinatti Opera *Art Director:* Amy Hildebrand

Victo Ngai
Title: Lucky Rooster 4 *Medium:* Mixed media
Size: 16 x 22 in. *Client:* Apple *Art Director:* Mesu Lu

Greg Ruth
Title: The Bride of Frankenstein
Medium: Graphite and digital *Size:* 24 x 36 in.
Client: Mondo *Art Director:* Eric Garza, Rob Jones and Mitch Putnam

Greg Ruth
Title: The Killing of a Sacred Deer
Medium: Graphite, color pencil and watercolor on paper *Size:* 24 x 36 in.
Client: Mondo *Art Director:* Eric Garza, Rob Jones and Mitch Putnam

Donato Giancola
Title: St. George and the White Dragon
Medium: Oil on panel *Size:* 30 x 24 in. *Client:* GenCon

Bayard Wu
Title: Crow *Medium:* Digital

Bayard Wu
Title: Ms. Hammer 4 *Medium:* Digital

Bayard Wu
Title: Come on! Jaime *Medium:* Digital

Anna Dittmann
Title: I Dreamt I Could Fly
Medium: Digital
Size: 12 x 12 in.
Client: Bert Loudis

Arantza Sestayo
Title: Oma *Medium:* Oil
Size: 18 ft. 90 in. x 13 ft. 78 in.

Craig Elliott
Title: Space Princess *Medium:* Digital
Size: 19 x 26 in. *Client:* gumroad.com/craigelliott

Alessandra Pisano
Title: Revelations *Medium:* Oil *Size:* 14 x 20 in. *Client:* Cu Dubh *Art Director:* David Macejka

Scott Gustafson
Title: Animal Crackers movie poster *Medium:* Oil on panel *Size:* 24 x 38 in.
Client: Blue Dream Studios *Art Director:* Scott Christian Sava *Designer:* Carter Goodrich

Bartosz Kosowski
Title: Chain Reaction
Medium: Digital
Size: 27 x 39 in.
Client: Studio Filmowe Kadr
Art Director: Bartosz Kosowski
Designer: Bartosz Kosowski

Jared Fiorino
Title: Jamo Gang
Medium: Graphite and photoshop
Size: 12 x 12 in.
Client: Jamo Gang

BOOK GOLD AWARD

VICTO NGAI
SERVING FISH

Medium: Mixed Media *Size:* 13 x 20 in.
Client: Fantastic Stories of the Imagination (FSI) *Art Director:* Nisi Shawl

"Winning a Spectrum *award is like riding a roller coaster of raw emotions: It's not good for the heart but may very well be worth having a heart attack for. Here are the five stages:*
1) Finding out about the nomination: delusion of grandeur
2) Checking out other nominated artwork: ego plummeted
3) Hand-crafted trophies revealed: desire ignited
4) Attending the ceremony: imposter syndrome triggered
5) Winning the award: extremely grateful yet humbled."

Victo Ngai is a Los Angeles-based illustrator from Hong Kong. "Victo" is neither a boy nor a typo but a nickname derived from Victoria, a leftover from the British colonization. Ngai's work has appeared in books, newspapers, magazines, advertisements and animations. Among her many clients are *The New York Times*, *The New Yorker*, *WSJ*, General Electric, Lufthansa, Johnnie Walker, Apple, IMAX, MTA Art and Design, McDonald's, Tor and Penguin Random House. Ngai is a *Forbes* "30 Under 30" honoree in Art and Style, a Society of Illustrators of New York and (newly minted) *Spectrum* gold medalist. She also has received numerous honors from American Illustration, the Art Directors Club, the Society for News Design, the Society of Publications Designers, *Communication Arts* and the British Science Fiction Association. She was a jury member for *Spectrum* 24 and is a current nominee for the 2018 Hugo Best Professional Artist and Locus Artist awards.

Cover art for *Dazzle Ships: World War I and the Art of Confusion*

BOOK SILVER AWARD

PETAR MESELDŽIJA
THE OLD MAN AND THE FOREST

Medium: Oils *Size:* 20.5 x 40.5 in. *Client:* Čarobna knjiga, Serbia

"Since the creation and the publication of my painting "The Old Man and the Forest," many have commented that it is perhaps the most spiritually charged work this fantasy artist has done until now.
I like to believe that their subjective opinion is objectively true. I am also happy that this particular painting has won a Spectrum award...this time not because of myself but because of the loving memory of my late wife.

"Now, imagine that you are able to put your head through this painting. Then turn your head to the left, and you will see a somewhat fragile-looking figure sitting on a bench some one hundred meters away.

"My wife fell seriously ill at the beginning of 2016, and fifteen months later she passed away. Her name was Anita. One beautiful sun-drenched October afternoon, we went for a little walk in the forest. Holding her walking stick in one hand, the other hand leaning on my arm, we walked slowly over a pretty forest path and after some time came across a clearing in the woods. There was a bench close to the path, so Anita sat down to rest. Touched by the beauty of the place, I went off the path to shoot some photos. These pictures were later used to create "The Old Man and the Forest." The totality and the sweetness of the moment—for all that was most precious to me was present in it—was the invisible driving force and the source of inspiration behind the creation of this piece.

"I have no doubt anymore that the essential element of this experience was love. It is love, in all its countless forms of expression, which is the hidden, incomprehensible essence of all our endeavors worthy of mention. The one who is able to understand love will know what art is."

Petar and Anita

The Old Recluse

Tommy Arnold
Title: Red Rising *Medium:* Digital *Client:* Subterranean Press *Art Director:* Yanni Kuznia

Wesley Burt
Title: A Girl & Her Friends—Monsters & Dames 2018 Benefit Book with Emerald City Comic-con *Medium:* Digital *Size:* 8 x 12 in.

Greg Manchess
Title: Heading Home, spread 118 *Medium:* Oil on linen *Size:* 15 x 37 in.
Client: Simon & Schuster/Saga Press *Art Director:* Greg Manchess *Designer:* Michael McCartney

Greg Manchess
Title: Airship Establishing Shot, spread 3
Medium: Oil on linen *Size:* 15 x 37 in. *Client:* Simon & Schuster/Saga Press *Art Director:* Greg Manchess *Designer:* Michael McCartney

Greg Manchess
Title: Empire Flyer, spread 31
Medium: Oil on linen *Size:* 15 x 37 in. *Client:* Simon & Schuster/Saga Press *Art Director:* Greg Manchess *Designer:* Michael McCartney

Greg Manchess
Title: Stellar Cartography, spread 75
Medium: Oil on linen *Size:* 15 x 37 in. *Client:* Simon & Schuster/Saga Press *Art Director:* Greg Manchess *Designer:* Michael McCartney

Greg Manchess
Title: Escape Into Forest, spread 101
Medium: Oil on linen *Size:* 15 x 37 in. *Client:* Simon & Schuster/Saga Press *Art Director:* Greg Manchess *Designer:* Michael McCartney

Daniel Dociu
Title: Nemesis Games/The Expanse
Medium: Digital *Client:* Subterranean Press *Art Director:* Yanni Kuznia

Jedd Chevrier
Title: Jungles of Chult *Medium:* Digital *Size:* 19.5 x 10 in. *Client:* Dungeons & Dragons/Wizards of the Coast *Art Director:* Kate Irwin

Edward Kinsella III
Title: Tea With Mom *Medium:* Colored pencil, ink, and gouache on paper
Size: 6.75 x 9.75 in. *Client:* Folio Society *Art Director:* Sheri Gee

Edward Kinsella III
Title: Drink Me *Medium:* Colored pencil, ink, gouache, and acryla gouache
Size: 6.75 x 9.75 in. *Client:* Folio Society *Art Director:* Sheri Gee

Jeffrey Alan Love
Title: Norse Myths: Tales of Odin, Thor and Loki
Medium: Acrylic and ink on paper
Size: 13 x 14 in. *Client:* Walker Books
Art Director: Ben Norland

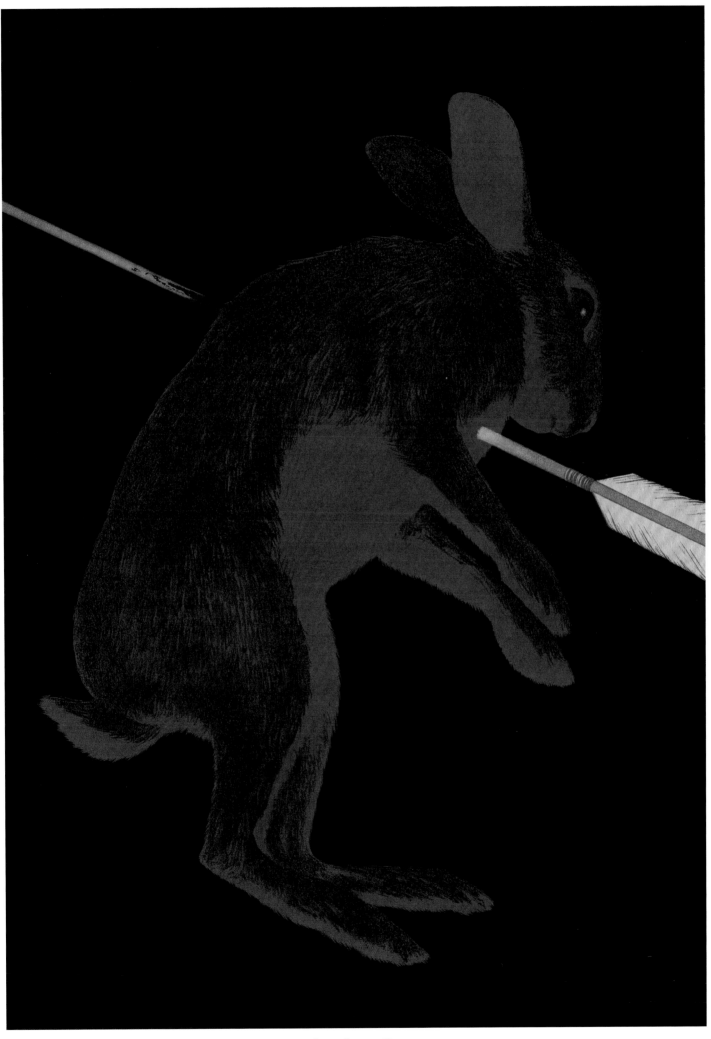

Edward Kinsella III
Title: The End of Innocence *Medium:* Colored pencil, ink, and gouache on paper *Size:* 6.75 x 9.75 in. *Client:* Folio Society *Art Director:* Sheri Gee

Alex Herrerias
Title: Arquimedes, Tot Principi Te un principi
Medium: Digital *Size:* 18.25 x 9.5 in. *Client:* Vegueta Edicions *Art Director:* Julio Fajardo *Designer:* Alicia Gómez

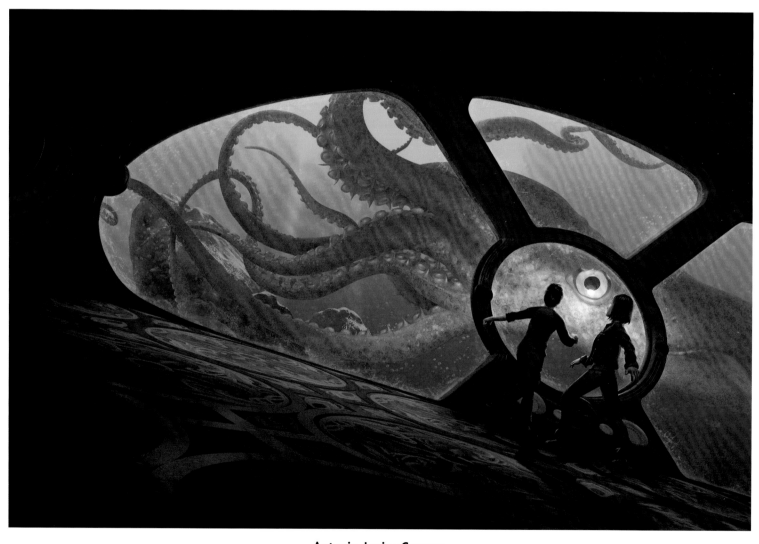

Antonio Javier Caparo
Title: Max Tilt, Fire the Depths *Medium:* Digital *Size:* 17.75 x 26.25 in. *Client:* Harper Collins *Art Director:* Andrea Vandergrift

Terryl Whitlatch
Title: Whookasai *Medium:* Pencil, marker and digital *Size:* 17 x 11 in. *Client:* Imagination International Inc. *Art Director:* Marianne Walker
© 2017 Imagination International Inc.

Roberto Pitturru
Title: Caravan Along the Chalk Road *Medium:* Digital *Size:* 18 x 5 in. *Client:* Monte Cook Games *Art Director:* Bear Weiter

Roch Urbaniak
Title: Cyclades *Medium:* Acrylic on canvas *Size:* 39 x 47 in.

Yuko Shimizu
Title: Oscar Wilde Fairytales: The Fisherman and his Soul
Medium: Ink drawing with digital color *Client:* Beehive Books
Art Director/Editor: Josh O'Neill

Yuko Shimizu
Title: Book cover for Tensorate Series 3: The Descent of Monsters
Medium: Ink drawing with digital color   *Client:* TOR   *Art Director:* Irene Gallo and Christine Foltzer

John Jude Palencar
Title: Deep Roots *Medium:* Acrylic on ragboard *Size:* 22 x 29 in. *Client:* TOR Books *Art Director:* Irene Gallo

Dominick Saponaro
Title: Echo of Things to Come
Medium: Digital *Size:* 6 x 9 in. *Client:* Orbit Books
Art Director: Lauren Panepinto *Designer:* Lauren Panepinto

Zoltan Boros
Title: Flying Monkey
Medium: Digital *Size:* 5 x 6.5 in.
Client: Dungeons & Dragons/Wizards of the Coast *Art Director:* Kate Irwin

Tim O'Brien
Title: OK Mr. Field
Medium: Oil on board *Size:* 12 x 16 in.
Client: Penguin *Art Director:* Christopher Brand

Anna and Elena Balbusso Twins
Title: Eclipse, cover art for the book "La metà del sole" by Daniela Morelli
Medium: Gouache, pencil, pen, collage and digital *Size:* 8.5 x 11.5 in.
Client: Edizioni Piemme Mondadori Group Italy *Art Director:* Fernando Ambrosi

Cory Godbey
Title: Messages *Medium:* White charcoal on toned paper
Size: 6 x 9 in.

Andrzej Lipczynski
Title: Chowanego *Medium:* Pencil *Size:* 8 x 12 in.

Anna and Elena Balbusso Twins
Title: "Le petit prince" by Antoine de Saint-Exupéry, children book
Medium: Gouache, pencil, pen and digital *Size:* 8.5 x 11.5 in. *Client:* Cideb De Agostini Group Italy *Art Director:* Nadia Maestri

Thomas Haller Buchanan
Title: "Royal Warrior" *Medium:* Mixed media *Size:* 13 x 18 in. *Client:* PAJ Publishing *Art Director:* Thomas Haller Buchanan

Thomas Haller Buchanan
Title: Sheherazade *Medium:* Mixed media
Size: 11 x 14 in. *Client:* PAJ Publishing *Art Director:* Thomas Haller Buchanan

Jie He (Mona)
Title: I Love You_Have Mutual Affinity *Size:* 12 in. *Client:* Forest Digital Art Studio

Mark A. Nelson
Title: Innsmouth: The Lost Drawings of Mannish Sycovia "Mayday"
Medium: Toned paper, coloured pencils and ink *Size:* 10 x 16 in. *Client:* Alaxis Press/GDP *Art Director:* Stephen Smith and Mark Nelson *Designer:* Stephen Smith

Sam Araya
Title: Journey to the Center of the Earth—The Fae
Medium: Digital *Client:* Easton Press *Art Director:* Michael Hendricks

Sam Araya
Title: The Ritual *Medium:* Digital *Client:* Tentacula

Sam Araya
Title: Journey to the center of the Earth—Key to the Enigma
Medium: Digital *Client:* Easton Press *Art Director:* Michael Hendricks

Sam Araya
Title: The Wendigo *Medium:* Digital *Client:* TOR.COM *Art Director:* Irene Gallo

Brom
Title: Stormbringer *Medium:* Oil *Size:* 22 x 28 in. *Client:* Centipede Press

Bastien Lecouffe Deharme
Title: Shaparaah *Medium:* Digital *Client:* GODS

Chris Cold and Bagriel Gray
Title: Rivenhome *Medium:* Digital *Size:* 10 x 6 in. *Client:* Monte Cook Games *Art Director:* Bear Weiter

Bastien Lecouffe Deharme
Title: Anackire *Medium:* Digital *Client:* DAW Books

Joy Yang
Title: The Fabric Merchant's Son *Medium:* Digital *Size:* 16 x 10 in.

Chris Dunn
Title: A Wise Old Owl
Medium: Watercolour and gouache
Size: 12 x 12 in. *Client:* Books Illustrated Ltd.
Art Director: Hilary Emeny

Chris Dunn
Title: Paisley Rabbit Book cover *Medium:* Watercolour and gouache *Size:* 17 x 22 in. *Client:* Impossible Dreams *Art Director:* Steve Richardson

Rovina Cai
Title: Tintinnabula: Trees *Medium:* Pencil and digital *Size:* 21.75 x 13 in. *Client:* Little Hare Books *Art Director:* Margrete Lamond

Rovina Cai
Title: Tintinnabula: Beasts *Medium:* Pencil and digital *Size:* 21.75 x 13 in. *Client:* Little Hare Books *Art Director:* Margrete Lamond

Rovina Cai
Title: Doorway *Medium:* Pencil and digital *Size:* 8.75 x 12.25 in. *Client:* Little Hare Books *Art Director:* Margrete Lamond

Julian Kok
Title: Temple of Lolth *Medium:* Digital *Client:* Wizards of the Coast *Art Director:* Kate Irwin

Tomasz Jedruszek
Title: After the War: Redemption's Blade *Medium:* Digital *Size:* 3535 x 5000 px.
Client: Rebellion *Art Director:* Jonathan Oliver
Copyrights by Rebellion Publishing Limited/Solaris Books

Micah Epstein
Title: The Last Sun *Medium:* Digital
Size: 6 x 8.75 in. *Client:* Pyr *Art Director:* Rene Sears

Lee Dotson
Title: AF/Angelarium   *Medium:* Digital
Size: 18 x 24 in.   *Client:* Peter Mohrbacher   *Art Director:* Peter Mohrbacher

Muhammad Mustafa
Title: The Journey of the Samovar   *Medium:* Mixed media and digital
Size: 12 x 8.5 in.   *Client:* Al Rewaq Publishing   *Art Director:* Muhammad Mustafa

Iris Compiet
Title: Banshee *Medium:* Watercolor and colored pencil on Arches paper *Size:* 18 x 9 in.
Artwork for book *Faeries of the Faultlines*

Iain McCaig
Title: Towan *Medium:* Watercolor *Size:* 28 x 21 in. *Client:* Expedition Art/Imagination International *Art Director:* Manny Carrasco

Iris Compiet
Title: Harry the Hobgoblin *Medium:* Watercolor and colored pencil on Arches paper *Size:* 8 x13 in.
Artwork for book *Faeries of the Faultlines*

Dan dos Santos
Title: Lightweaver *Medium:* Acrylic and colored pencil *Size:* 20 x 30 in. *Client:* Brandon Sanderson *Art Director:* Isaac Stewart

Dan dos Santos
Title: The Name of the Wind: The Archives
Medium: Acrylic and colored pencil *Size:* 10 x 15 in.
Client: DAW Books *Art Director:* Betsy Wollheim

Dan dos Santos
Title: Witchy Eye *Medium:* Oil and digital *Size:* 12 x 18 in.
Client: Baen Books *Art Director:* Toni Weisskopf

Eric Belisle
Title: Eladrin, Winter
Medium: Digital *Size:* 11.5 x 16 in.
Client: Dungeons & Dragons/Wizards of the Coast *Art Director:* Kate Irwin

David Plunkert
Title: Frankenstein's Dream from "Frankenstein: The 200th Anniversary Edition"
Medium: Digital mixed media *Size:* 7.5 x 9 in. *Client:* Rockpor

Yoann Lossel
Title: Beowulf—Grendel's Mother
Medium: Mixed media on Arches paper: graphite, hydrangeas petals
and gold leaf (24k) *Client:* Easton Press *Art Director:* Michael Hendricks

David Palumbo
Title: The Little Mothers
Medium: Oil on panel
Size: 16 x 24 in.
Client: Centipede Press Art
Art Director: Jerad Walters

Yoann Lossel
Title: Beowulf—Grendel's Mother Mere *Medium:* Mixed media on Arches paper: graphite, hydrangeas petals, gold (24k), silver and copper leaf
Size: 12 x 16 in. *Client:* Easton Press *Art Director:* Michael Hendricks

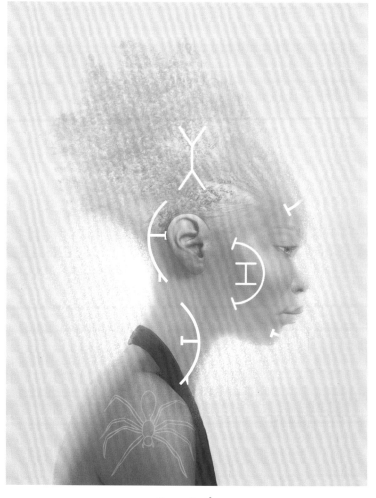

Victo Ngai
Title: Clover *Medium:* Mixed media
Size: 13 x 19 in. *Client:* Tor.com *Art Director:* Irene Gallo

Greg Ruth
Title: Sunni and the Mysteries of Osisi
Medium: Graphite, color pencil and digital *Size:* 10 x 12 in.
Client: Cassava Republic *Art Director:* Bibi Bakare Yousef

J.A.W. Cooper
Title: Familiars *Client:* Flesk Publications

J.A.W. Cooper
Title: Flora And Fauna *Client:* Flesk Publications

J.A.W. Cooper
Title: Viscera *Client:* Flesk Publications

Tommy Arnold
Title: Void Black Shadow *Medium:* Digital
Client: Tor.com Publishing *Art Director:* Christine Foltzer

Tommy Arnold
Title: Shadowborn *Medium:* Digital *Client:* Orbit Books
Art Director: Lauren Panepinto *Designer:* Kirk Benshoff and Lauren Panepinto

Sebastian Kowoll
Title: First Keeper *Medium:* Digital *Size:* 8 x 12 in. *Client:* Steven Kelliher

Tommy Arnold
Title: Ghostly Chords *Medium:* Digital *Client:* Edward Giordano

Tommy Arnold
Title: Killing Gravity *Medium:* Digital *Client:* Tor.com Publishing *Art Director:* Christine Foltzer

Olly Lawson
Title: Tu'narath *Medium:* Digital *Size:* 8.5 x 6 in. *Client:* Dungeons & Dragons/Wizards of the Coast *Art Director:* Kate Irwin

Petar Meseldžija
Title: The Vision of Novak the Blacksmith *Medium:* Oils *Size:* 23.50 x 39.5 in. *Client:* Čarobna knjiga, Serbia

Petar Meseldžija
Title: The Sentinel *Medium:* Oils *Size:* 19.75 x 29.25 in. *Client:* Čarobna knjiga, Serbia

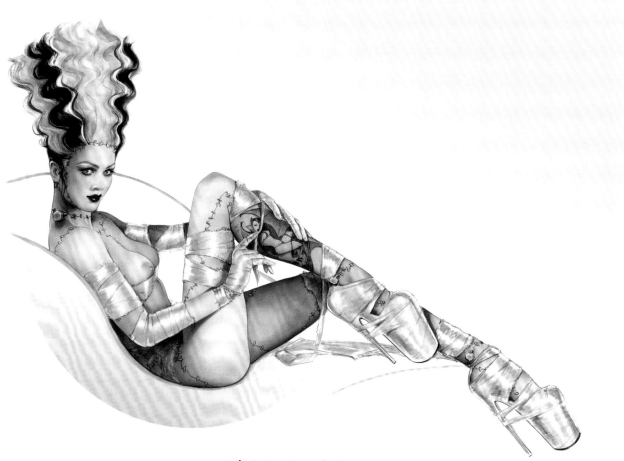

Olivia De Berardinis
Title: Franky's Bride *Medium:* Watercolor and gouache on lanaquerrele watercolor *Size:* 30 x 22.5 in. *Client:* Self *Art Director:* Olivia *Designer:* Olivia

Erica Williams
Title: Witchborn by Nicholas Bowling
Medium: Ink and digital color *Size:* 5 x 8 in. *Client:* Chicken House Publishing
Art Director: Rachel Hickman *Designer:* Erica Williams

Josh Tufts
Title: Her Majesty *Medium:* Pencil and digital
Size: 10 x 13.75 in. *Client:* Blue Willow Press *Art Director:* Scott Raudnest

Olivia De Berardinis
Title: Tiger Lili *Medium:* Acrylic on wood panel *Size:* 20 x 20 in. *Client:* Self *Art Director:* Olivia *Designer:* Olivia

John Howe
Title: The Making of Middle-Earth *Medium:* Watercolor *Size:* 28 x 18 in. *Client:* HarperCollins *Art Director:* Chris Smith

Beatriz Martin Vidal
Title: Conversation *Medium:* Oil on BFK Rives *Size:* 22 x 14 in. *Client:* Thule Editions *Art Director:* Jose Diaz

Wayne Reynolds
Title: Desperate Ritual *Medium:* Acrylic on artboard *Size:* 10.5 x 7.75 in. *Client:* Wizards of the Coast *Art Director:* Dawn Murin

William O'Connor
Title: Beowulf's Battle *Medium:* Oil and digital *Size:* 21 x 34 in. *Client:* F&W Mediav *Designer:* Clare Finney

David Wenzel
Title: The Hall of Dragons *Medium:* Watercolor *Size:* 21 x 11.5 in. *Client:* IDW *Art Director:* David Wenzel

Donato Giancola
Title: Dwarf Merchants *Medium:* Pencil and chalk on paper
Size: 14 x 11 in. *Client:* Dwarven Forge

Donato Giancola
Title: Kvothe—The Name of Things *Medium:* Oil on Panel
Size: 24 x 18 in. *Client:* Argo *Art Director:* Martin Sust

David Wenzel
Title: The Dowry *Medium:* Watercolor *Size:* 11.5 x 16.25 in. *Client:* IDW *Art Director:* David Wenzel

Scott Gustafson
Title: Carpet to Adventure *Medium:* Oil on panel *Size:* 14 x 18 in. *Client:* Tom Bancroft

Scott Gustafson

Top:
Title: The Boy Meets the North Wind
opening spread
Medium: Oil on panel
Size: 25 x 10 in.
Client: Artisan Books
Art Director: Scott Gustafson

Bottom:
Title: The Mice in Council
Medium: Oil on canvas
Size: 14 x 18 in.
Client: Artisan Books
Art Director: Scott Gustafson

Annie Stegg Gerard
Title: The Angel of Music/The Phantom of the Opera *Medium:* Oil on canvas
Size: 12 x 16 in. *Client:* Easton Press *Art Director:* Michael Hendricks

Justin Gerard
Title: The Taking of the Silmarils *Medium:* Graphite and digital *Size:* 12 x 18 in.

Cory Trego-Erdner
Title: Marut *Medium:* Digital *Size:* 3.5 x 4 in.
Client: Dungeons & Dragons/Wizards of the Coast *Art Director:* Kate Irwin

Justin Gerard
Title: The Flight from Doriath *Medium:* Watercolor and digital *Size:* 16 x 20 in.

Peter Diamond
Title: Hansel & Gretel—Into The Oven *Medium:* Ink and digital *Size:* 9 x 12 in. *Client:* Amazon Publishing *Art Director:* Tyler Freidenrich

Peter Diamond
Title: Hansel & Gretel—Abandoned
Medium: Ink, graphite and digital *Size:* 9 x 12 in.
Client: Amazon Publishing *Art Director:* Tyler Freidenrich

Peter Diamond
Title: Hansel & Gretel—Knusper, Knusper, Knaueschen
Medium: Ink and digital *Size:* 9 x 12 in.
Client: Amazon Publishing *Art Director:* Tyler Freidenrich

Johan Grenier
Title: Extremis Chamber *Medium:* Digital/photoshop *Client:* Games workshop *Art Director:* Darius Hinks
© Copyright Games Workshop Limited 2018

John Petersen
Title: Setting *Medium:* Graphite and digital
Size: 6 x 9 in. *Client:* Monte Cook Games, LLC *Art Director:* Bear Weiter

John Anthony Di Giovanni
Title: Ghosts of Tomorrow
Medium: Digital *Size:* 12 x 18 in. *Client:* Michael R. Fletcher

Daren Bader
Title: Mountain Demons *Medium:* Digital *Size:* 8.5 x 11 in. *Client:* Modiphius Entertainment

COMICS GOLD AWARD

ALEX ALICE
CASTLE IN THE STARS BOOK 2, PAGES 60-61

Medium: Pencil and inks on illustration board *Size:* 30 x 20 in.
Client: Rue de Sèvres/First Second *Art Director:* Nadia Gibert

"Hope and solace: I'm very glad that the jury chose this moment for the award. This is a great honor for me, as the page has a special place in my heart."

Alex Alice is a graphic novel writer and artist, working in France and sometimes in the U.S.
Born in 1974, he grew up in the south of France and had the chance to travel around Europe, where he developed a lifelong passion for the ruins and castles of the medieval and romantic ages. This infused his art—from the grim medieval setting of the esoteric thriller The Third Testament (1997-2003, co-written with Xavier Dorison) to the primeval mythic world of Siegfried (2007-2011), an operatic retelling of the northern saga of the great dragon-slayer.

Alice's interests range from cinema and animation to painting and illustration (he received two Spectrum awards for his covers) and extend to fine art and sculpture. He exhibited Siegfried-related pieces with French sculptor Christophe Charbonnel in 2015. His Siegfried also has been produced as a video performance set to Wagner's music and performed by the Orchestre National de Lyon.

His current ongoing series, Castle in the Stars, is the artist's most personal work to date. In it, Alice draws on Jules Verne and nineteenth-century romanticism to create a watercolor world of adventure and wonder that enchants adults and younger readers alike. A special exhibition on this series was produced in 2017 by the Angoulême International Comics festival, showcasing seventy pieces of original art along with costumes, props and models.

Photo by Isabelle Franciosa

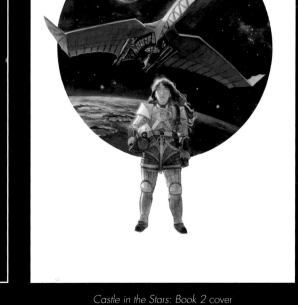

Castle in the Stars: Book 2 cover

GARY GIANNI
HELLBOY: INTO THE SILENT SEA, PAGE 11

Medium: Pen and ink *Size:* 12 x 18 in. *Client:* Dark Horse

"This award represents a community of artists that I'm continually in awe of. It's an honor to receive it."

Gary Gianni attended the Chicago Academy of Fine Arts in the 1970s. He was fortunate to have received some solid instruction along the way and developed lifelong friendships with fellow students Geof Darrow and Scott Gustafson. His early career included working as a newspaper editorial artist and a courtroom sketch reporter for television, where he covered the trial of serial killer John Wayne Gacy in 1980. Throughout the 1980s he illustrated books and magazines, and in 1990 he adapted and drew his first work in the comic-book field: a Classics Illustrated version of the tales of O. Henry. Since then, Gianni has alternated his career between the two art forms, as a book illustrator and a comic-book artist. In comics, he has worked with talents such as Archie Goodwin, Alan Moore, Harlan Ellison, John Cullen Murphy, Mark Schultz, Michael Kaluta and Mike Mignola. His book illustrations are found in the novels of H.P. Lovecraft, R.E. Howard, Ray Bradbury, Michael Chabon and George R.R. Martin. For nine years, Gianni illustrated the newspaper comic strip *Prince Valiant*. He also wrote and illustrated *The MonsterMen Mysteries*, which appeared as a backup feature in the *Hellboy* comics.

E. M. Gist
Title: Kratos *Medium:* Oil on panel *Size:* 14 x 22 in. *Client:* Dark Horse Comics *Art Director:* Spencer Cushing

Paolo Rivera
Title: Shirtless Bear Fighter #4 Variant cover *Medium:* Gouache and digital
Size: 11 x 17 in. *Client:* Fuzzy Wipes, LLC *Art Director:* Jody LeHeup *Designer:* Manny Mederos © Fuzzy Wipes, LLC

Xaviere Daumarie
Title: Ugly Cinderwench and the Very Angry Ghost, page 3 *Medium:* Ink and digital *Size:* 7 x 10.5 in. *Client:* TO Comix Press *Art Director:* Allison O'To

Xaviere Daumarie
Title: Ugly Cinderwench and the Very Angry Ghost, page 1
Medium: Ink and digital *Size:* 7 x 10.5 in.
Client: TO Comix Press *Art Director:* Allison O'Toole

Xaviere Daumarie
Title: Ugly Cinderwench and the Very Angry Ghost, page 4
Medium: Ink and digital *Size:* 7 x 10.5 in.
Client: TO Comix Press *Art Director:* Allison O'Toole

Alex Alice
Title: Castle in the Stars Book 3 Special Edition
Medium: Pencil and inks on illustration board
Size: 30 x 30 in. *Client:* Rue de Sèvres
Art Director: Nadia Gibert

Paolo Rivera
Title: Hellboy and the B.P.R.D.: 1955 Occult Intelligence #1
Medium: Gouache and acrylic *Size:* 13 x 19 in.
Client: Dark Horse Comics *Art Director:* Scott Allie © Mike Mignola

Lucio Parrillo
Title: Venom vs Black Cat #160 cover
Medium: Oil painting *Size:* 19 x 27 in. *Client:* Marvel Comics

Terry Dodson
Title: Astonishing X-Men #1
Medium: Pen and ink and digital *Size:* 12 x 18 in. *Client:* Marvel Comics
Art Director: Christina Harrington *Inker:* Rachel Dodson *Colorist:* Terry Dodson

Terry Dodson
Title: Star Wars 38 *Medium:* Pen and ink and digital *Size:* 12 x 18 in.
Client: Marvel Comics *Art Director:* Heather Antos/Lucas Film *Inker:* Rachel Dodson *Colorist:* Terry Dodson

Kaare Andrews
Title: Darth Maul 5 variant cover
Medium: Acrylic and mixed *Size:* 40 x 30 in. *Client:* Marvel comics

Mike Mayhew
Title: Star Wars: Storms of Crait #1, page 24
Medium: Pencil with digital color *Size:* 6.5 x 10.25 in.
Client: Marvel Comics *Art Director:* Jordan White *Art Designer:* Mike Mayhew

Mike Mayhew
Title: Star Wars: Storms of Crait #1, page 25 *Medium:* Pencil with digital color
Size: 6.5 x 10.25 in. *Client:* Marvel Comics *Art Director:* Jordan White *Art Designer:* Mike Mayhew

Frank Cho
Title: Lost World *Medium:* Ballpoint pen and colored ink
Size: 14 x 21 in. *Client:* Dynamite *Art Director:* Frank Cho *Designer:* Frank Cho

Frank Cho
Title: Skybourne Collection Cover *Size:* 14 x 21 in. *Client:* BOOM! Studios
Art Director: Frank Cho *Designer:* Frank Cho *Colorist:* Sabine Rich

Frank Cho
Title: Harley Quinn #23 cover *Medium:* Pen, ink, and digital colors *Size:* 19 x 24 in.
Client: DC Comics *Art Director:* Mark Chiarello *Designer:* Frank Cho *Colorist:* Sabine Rich

Jeffrey Alan Love
Title: Head Lopper *Medium:* Acrylic and ink on paper *Size:* 10 x 15 in. *Client:* Image Comics *Art Director:* Andrew MacLean

Gary Gianni
Title: Hellboy, page 15 *Medium:* Pen and ink
Size: 12 x 18 in. *Client:* Dark Horse

Gary Gianni
Title: Hellboy, page 21 *Medium:* Pen and ink
Size: 12 x 18 in. *Client:* Dark Horse

Jeremy A. Bastian
Title: Alternate Cover for Judas issue #1
Medium: Pencil and micron *Size:* 7.25 x 10.75 in.
Client: BOOM! Studios *Designer:* Jeremy A. Bastian

Sarah Webb
Title: Kochab *Medium:* Watercolor and digital *Size:* 14 x 10.5 in.

Kellan Jett
Title: Mega City Region *Medium:* Digital *Client:* Studio Bean *Art Director:* Michael Molinari

Cory Godbey
Title: Jim Henson's The Dark Crystal Tales
Medium: Watercolor and digital
Client: The Jim Henson Co./BOOM/Archaia
Art Director: Sierra Hahn and Cameron Chittock

Yuko Shimizu
Title: The Highest House covers issue #1 and #3
Medium: Ink drawing with digital color   *Client:* IDW Publishing
Art Director: Denton Tipton, Mike Carey and Peter Gross

Bastien Lecouffe Deharme
Title: Cymoril's Dream *Medium:* Digital *Client:* Glenat

David Palumbo
Title: Showdown *Medium:* Oil on panel
Size: 16 x 24 in. *Client:* Dark Horse Comics *Art Director:* Scott Allie

Kirt Burdick
Title: Fae Archaic *Medium:* Graphite pencil and digital *Size:* 11 x 17 in.

David Palumbo
Title: Possession *Medium:* Oil on panel
Size: 16 x 24 in. *Client:* Dark Horse Comics *Art Director:* Scott Allie

David Palumbo

Title: Rats! *Medium:* Oil on panel *Size:* 16 x 24 in. *Client:* Dark Horse Comics *Art Director:* Scott Allie

Daxue Ding
Title: Crossroad *Medium:* Hand painted *Size:* 25.75 x 35.5 in.

Andy Brase
Title: Punisher: The Platoon #1 cover
Medium: Pen and ink *Size:* 11 x 17 in. *Client:* Marvel Comics

Hayden Sherman
Title: Wasted Space #1 cover *Medium:* Pencil, watercolor and digital *Size:* 14 x 11 in. *Client:* Vault Comics

Hayden Sherman
Title: The Few, trade cover *Medium:* Ink and digital *Size:* 6.75 x 10.5 in. *Client:* Image Comics

Goñi Montes
Title: The Fool for Sword Quest *Medium:* Digital *Size:* 7 x 10.5 in.
Client: Dynamite Entertainment *Art Director:* Kevin Ketner

Scott M. Fischer
Title: Angel #10 *Medium:* Digital
Client: Dark Horse Comics *Art Director:* Freddye Miller

Stephen Player
Title: Witchunt *Medium:* Digital *Size:* 17.75 x 17.75 in.

Daniel Dociu
Title: Pilgrims/Mystical Places *Medium:* Digital
Client: Amazon Game Studios *Art Director:* Daniel Dociu

Steve Rude
Title: Future Quest Showcase #1 *Medium:* Watercolor and prismacolor pencil *Size:* 20 x 29 in. *Client:* DC Comics *Art Director:* Brittany Holtzer

CONCEPT ART GOLD AWARD

WANGJIE LI
BATTLEFIELD SCENE

Medium: Photoshop   *Size:* 12 x 6 in.   *Client:* Blnk Creative LLC   *Designer:* Wangjie Li

"It is with great pleasure that I receive this award, and this is a great encouragement to me."

Wangjie Li is a visual artist who enjoys making concept art and illustrations. With over eight years of professional experience, he has worked with projects such as Wizards of the Coast, The Elder Scrolls Online, Lineage II and Legend of the Cryptids. Aside from being a concept artist, Li also has been an art instructor since 2010. He enjoys assisting other young artists in preparing their school portfolios and future careers. He decided to put his class online in 2014 to learn more about online education.

Born and raised in southern China, Wangjie Li obtained his Bachelor of Animation degree at Hunan International Economics University in 2012. He also is currently a graduate student in fine art at the Academy of Art University in San Francisco.

CONCEPT ART SILVER AWARD

ANTHONY FRANCISCO
OKOYE AND NAKIA THE DORA MILAJE

Size: 13 x 19 in.   *Client:* Marvel Studios   *Art Director:* Ryan Meinerding

"Thank you, Spectrum and the Spectrum 25 judges for this award! I have never won anything like this in my life. I feel fortunate that for eighteen years I had a chance to do art and live well. It was a hard struggle but I was always positive in my outlook and lucky enough to have friends and family who helped me improve as an artist and as a person every single day."

Anthony Francisco has been a concept artist and an art director for films and videogames for eighteen years. He is currently the Senior Visual Development Concept Illustrator at Marvel Studios. Francisco helps with designing the heroes and villains for the Marvel cinematic universe. He was fortunate enough to have designed one of Marvel's most beloved characters for the big screen: Baby Groot! His other iconic characters include Loki for *Thor: Ragnarok* and the costumes for the Dora Milaje (Okoye and Nakia) for *Black Panther*. Francisco also has worked on all three volumes of *Guardians of the Galaxy, Captain Marvel, Avengers: Infinity War, Antman, Antman and the Wasp,* and *Doctor Strange.*

Wesley Burt
Title: Transformers 5 Autobot Design—'Canopy' *Medium:* Digital *Size:* 10 x 14 in. *Client:* Paramount Pictures, Bay Films *Art Director:* Michael Bay and Jeffrey Beecroft

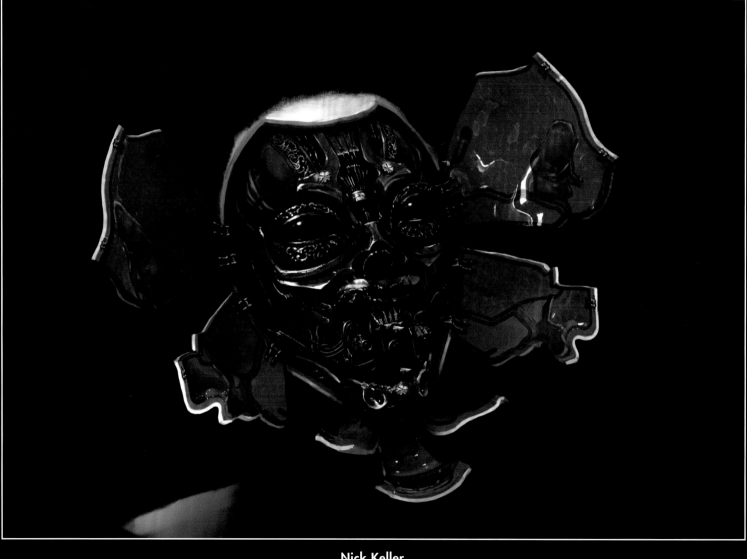

Nick Keller
Title: Geisha Interior (Ghost in the Shell) *Medium:* Digital *Client:* Amblin Partners *Art Director:* Weta Workshop

Nick Keller
Title: Kuze Geisha (Ghost in the Shell) *Medium:* Digital
Client: Amblin Partners *Art Director:* Weta Workshop

Eddie Mendoza
Title: Agent Orange

Te Hu
Title: Buddha Wenshu *Medium:* Digital

Wangjie Li
Title: Unexpectable Meeting *Medium:* Photoshop *Size:* 12 x 8.5 in. *Client:* Blnk Creative LLC *Designer:* Wangjie Li

Wangjie Li
Title: Ladakh Girl *Medium:* Photoshop *Size:* 12 x 9.5 in. *Client:* IE_Art Studio *Designer:* Wangjie Li

Theo Prins
Title: Road/Guild Wars 2 Concept 3 *Medium:* Digital *Client:* Guild Wars 2, ArenaNet *Art Director:* Horia Dociu

Theo Prins
Title: Free City of Amnoon *Medium:* Digital *Client:* Guild Wars 2, ArenaNet *Art Director:* Horia Dociu

Zhengyi Wang
Title: Elon Riverlands *Medium:* Digital *Client:* ArenaNet *Art Director:* Daniel Dociu

Wayne Haag
Title: Alien Covenant Concept Art 03—Juggernaut Wreck *Medium:* Digital *Size:* 13.5 x 5.5 in. *Client:* 20th Century Fox Studios *Production Designer:* Chris Seagers

Dong Lee
Title: Pirate transport *Medium:* Photoshop and modo *Size:* 50 x 26.25 in.

Samuel Alexander
Title: Discovery *Medium:* Digital *Size:* 16 x 9 in. *Client:* Imaginary Forces *Art Director:* Sam Alexander *Designer:* Sam Alexander

Paul Bonner
Title: Trudvang, Bard *Medium:* Water colour *Size:* 17.75 x 14.25 in. *Client:* Riotminds *Art Director:* Theo Bergquist

Paul Bonner
Title: Mittlander *Medium:* Water colour *Size:* 16 x 9 in. *Client:* Riotminds *Art Director:* Theo Bergquist

Paul Bonner
Title: Trudvang, Priest
Medium: Water colour
Size: 19.25 x 14.5 in.
Client: Riotminds
Art Director: Theo Bergquist

Kellan Jett
Title: Mirror Portal *Medium:* Digital *Client:* Devon Stern *Art Director:* Devon Stern

Kellan Jett
Title: Veil of Hume 2 *Medium:* Digital *Client:* Devon Stern *Art Director:* Devon Stern

Kellan Jett
Title: Deva Urban Building *Medium:* Digital *Client:* MTB Design Works *Art Director:* Marc Ten Bosch

David Greco
Title: Eternal Love *Medium:* Digital *Size:* 15 x 20 in. *Client:* Crowfall—ArtCraft Entertainment *Art Director:* Melissa Preston

Olivia De Berardinis
Title: Queen's Embrace: Variant *Medium:* Acrylic on maple wood panel *Size:* 30 x 20 in. *Client:* Sideshow Collectibles *Art Director:* Tom Gilliland *Designer:* Olivia

Carlyn Lim
Title: Undead Army/Guild Wars 2: Path of Fire *Medium:* Digital *Size:* 12 x 7.5 in. *Client:* ArenaNet *Art Director:* Daniel Dociu *Designer:* Carlyn Lim

Ed Binkley
Title: Tomb of the Djinn *Medium:* Digital painting *Size:* 20 x 15 in.

Adam Volker
Title: Manifest 99: Bear *Medium:* Digital illustration *Size:* 12 x 5.5 in. *Client:* Flight School *Art Director:* Adam Volker *Designer:* Jake Wyatt

Gustavo Mendonca
Title: Ink Tales *Medium:* Pen and ink and digital *Size:* 13 x 19 in. *Client:* Gus Mendonca Design LLC *Art Director:* Gustavo Mendonca

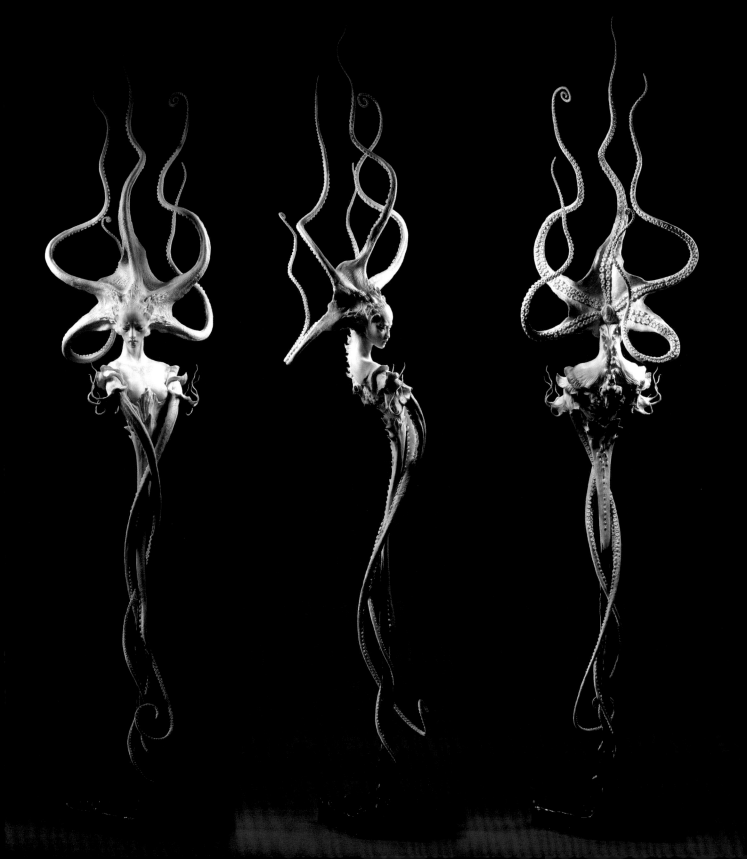

DIMENISONAL GOLD AWARD

FOREST ROGERS
OCTOPOID DESCENDING

Medium: Kato polyclay, garnets, wood, aluminum and stainless wire
Size: 43 in.   *Client:* Illuxcon   *Photographer:* Dave Snow

"Ms Octopoid and I are incredibly honored, for there is so much mystery, charm and genius in this field now that we swim in a veritable sea of wonders. I consider myself astonishingly lucky to have found this world to dwell in. It is so richly illuminated by colleagues and friends that it seems to me we have our very own Golden Age. It brings things into being that would never otherwise exist, as does the enthusiasm of those who created Spectrum for us and those who love the works we create. That's the other vital part of the dance. Thank you!

"My artist mother, Lou P. Rogers, surrounded me with alien marvels from the very beginning, so finding Spectrum has been a kind of coming home. Mine has been an eccentric road. I studied stage design at Carnegie-Mellon University. Armed with an MFA in costume design, I sculpted nude dinosaur prototypes for a major natural-history museum. (If you played with plastic dinos in your youth, we may have met by proxy.) Working rigorously with paleontologists was grounding in a way that still guides me even in the realm of the fantastic. Painting nine-foot angels in the dome of a Russian Orthodox cathedral gave me something numinous in memory. Add a childhood passion for the illustrated books of the Golden Age, and now the gobsmacking magic of my artist colleagues in this fantastic field, and my inspirations are clear. Oh! Octopoid Descending wants me to mention working with a certain aquarium on their giant squid toy prototype. She feels it gives her a certain gravitas. Does she also want me to mention the strawberry-scented, squid-shaped eraser I once helped create? One cannot be sure…"

Night Bloom

DIMENSIONAL SILVER AWARD

JESSICA DALVA
I'LL NEED ENTIRE CITIES TO REPLACE YOU

Medium: Mixed media sculpture *Size:* 16 x 20 x 4 in. *Client:* Arch Enemy Arts Gallery

"I am completely floored to have won this award. I'm floored just to be included in Spectrum. *To be selected out of so many applicants by a panel of artists that I admire so much is such an unbelievable honor. The intention behind this piece was to serve as a reminder and motivation for myself to keep striving for the best I can achieve and not to shy away from seeking adventure and risk. Receiving the award for this particular piece is especially meaningful for me, as it reassures me that the direction I am headed is the right one."*

Jessica Dalva is a sculptor and fabricator living and working in Northern California. Her experiences in stop-motion animation, costume creation and illustration influence her three-dimensional work, in which she uses a variety of materials and techniques. Dalva's sculptural work began to take shape at Otis College of Art and Design in Los Angeles, where she earned her BFA in illustration. In the years since, her work in a myriad of industries (and peculiarly curious projects) has allowed her to develop unique methods of combining disparate techniques in order to produce haunting and illustrative sculptures. She currently is focused on creating pieces for a number of galleries across the country and abroad, as well as working as a freelance fabricator.

Growing up in the California Bay Area, Dalva has been immersed in both art and nature since birth. Her mother and father, being artists themselves (a sculptor and a filmmaker, respectively), have been tremendous influences on both her journey as an artist and the lens through which she sees the world. They have always been endlessly encouraging of her desires to draw, sculpt and create any strange little thing her mind could dream up, all while imparting a deep appreciation of the natural world—an appreciation that continually surfaces in her work.

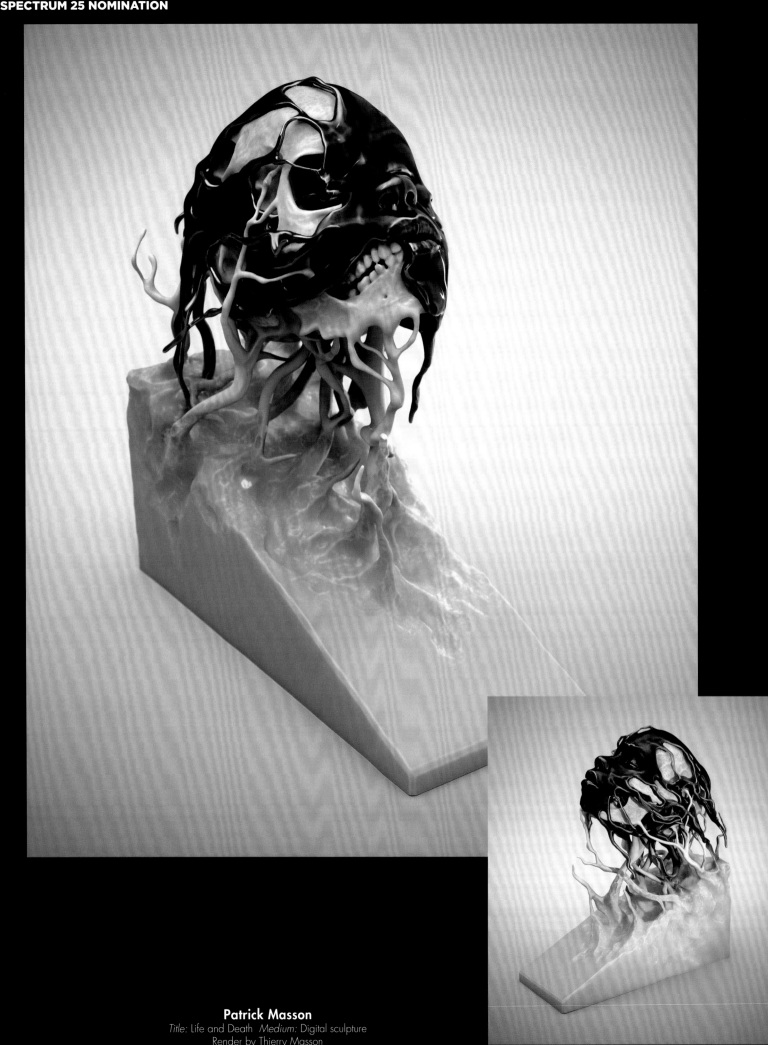

Patrick Masson
Title: Life and Death *Medium:* Digital sculpture
Render by Thierry Masson

DopePope
Title: Cthulhu 22 Inch Tall Statue *Medium:* Digital sculpture in ZBrush *Client:* Pop Culture Shock Collectibles *Art Director:* Jerry Macaluso

AKIHITO

Title: Statue of Peace *Medium:* Fiberglass *Size:* 67 x 22 x 20 in. *Client:* AKIHITO *Art Director:* AKIHITO *Designer:* Yuichi Ito

Jessica Dalva
Title: Come With Me and I'll Tell You Everything   *Medium:* Mixed media sculpture
Size: 19 x 12 x 10 in.   *Client:* La Luz de Jesus Gallery

Forest Rogers
Title: The Sphinx And The Hermit
Medium: Japanese air-dry clay, mulberry paper and wood
Size: 8 x 25.5 in.   *Photographer:* Dave Snow

Patrick Masson
Title: Tinkerbell   *Medium:* Polymer clay (fimo)
Size: 1.25 x 3.5 x 5 in.   *Client:* Blacksmith Miniatures
From an original illustration by Jean-Baptiste Monge

Patrick Masson
Title: Hate Um'Kator Prince
Medium: Polymer clay (fimo) and epoxy (magic sculp)   *Size:* 2 x 2.75 in.
Client: CMoN for HATE The Board Game   *Art Director:* Mike McVey
From an original illustration by Adrian Smith

Dug Stanat
Title: Koshchei: I Am a Long Way From Death   *Medium:* Mixed media   *Size:* 25 x 8 x 9 in.

Dug Stanat
Title: The Meat Picker *Medium:* Mixed media *Size:* 10 x 6 x 6 in.

Goushi
Title: Go-Shintai *Medium:* Washi and mixed media
Size: 27 x 19 x 11 in. *Client:* Non *Art Director:* Goushi *Designer:* Goushi

AKIHITO
Title: Valkyrie *Medium:* White casting resin, wood and Rigid foam *Size:* 35 x 42 x 13 in. *Client:* AKIHITO *Art Director:* AKIHITO *Designer:* AKIHITO

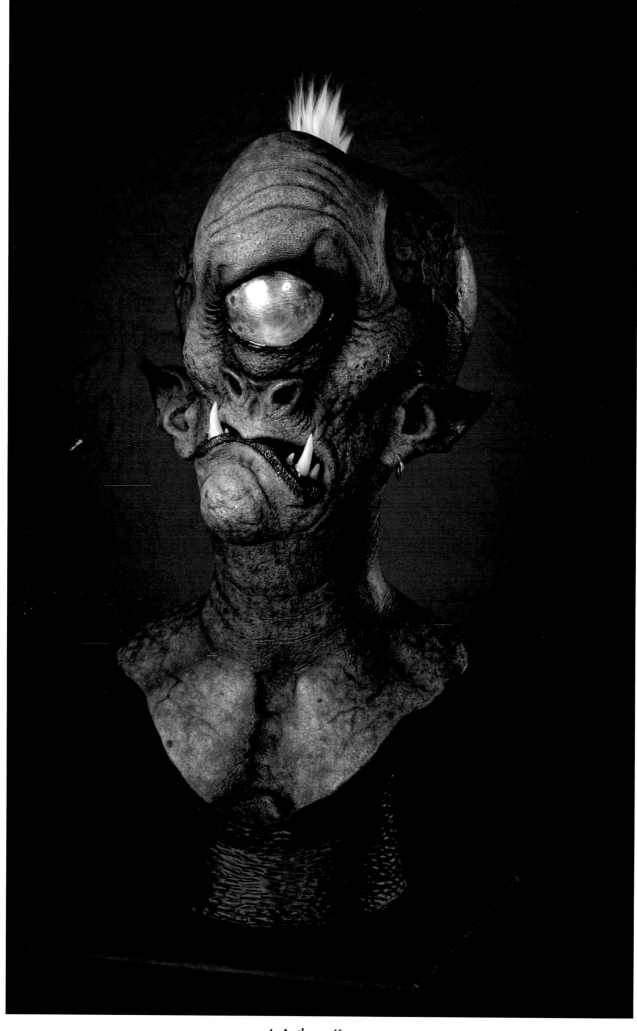

J. Anthony Kosar
Title: U-Logy *Medium:* Poly-foam filled latex and acrylic paint *Size:* 10.5 x 23 x 10.5 in. *Photographer:* Bear McGivney

Kosart Studios
Title: Aleon & Aleen *Medium:* Poly-foam filled latex and acrylic paint
Size: Aleon: 12 x 15 x 13 in./Aleen: 11 x 13 x 12 in. *Client:* Adobe *Art Director:* J. Anthony Kosar *Photographer:* Bear McGivney

Allan Diego Carrasco
Title: 40 Days Dans Le Desert *Medium:* Polymer Clay, acrylic paints and wood *Size:* 10 x 8 in. *Client:* MUMI—Museum of Miniatures *Designer:* Moebius Jean Giraud

157

Virginie Ropars
Title: Acanthophis V Medium: Mixed media
Size: 26.75 crown closed, 28.75 crown opened

Virginie Ropars
Title: Blue Bird Medium: Mixed media

James Shoop
Title: David Crockett Lion of the West Study
Medium: Original hand sculpture wax study *Size:* 24 x 12 x 10 in.
Client: Shoop Sculptural Design Inc. *Art Director:* James Shoop

Allan Diego Carrasco
Title: Embodying a Spirit
Medium: Polymer Clay, fiber, feathers, shell and acrylic paint *Size:* 12 in.

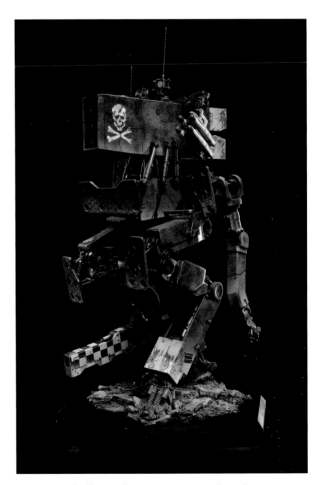

Leonard Ellis, Jules German, and Joel Savage
Title: Grey Wolf (Giant Killer Robots) *Medium:* Cast urethane resin
Size: 15 x 8.25 x 9.75 in. *Art Director:* Weta Workshop
3D Designer: Joel Savage *Modelmaker:* Leonard Ellis *Painter:* Jules German

Thomas S. Kuebler
Title: Old Scratch *Medium:* Silicone and mixed media *Size:* 25 x 67 in.

Joel Harlow with Leonard Macdonald
Title: Uncle Creepy *Medium:* Silicone, resin, foam, acrylic and hair
Client: Morphology Inc. *Art Director:* Joel Harlow *Designer:* Joel Harlow

Dan Chudzinski
Title: Flea Flicker *Medium:* Resin and mixed media sculpture
Size: 16 x 14 x 12 in. *Photographer:* David Casperson

Jamie Beswarick
Title: Gollum (The Lord of the Rings)
Medium: Sculpted in clay, recreated with resin, leather
Size: 13 x 16.5 x 13 in. *Art Director:* Weta Workshop
Principal Sculptor: Jamie Beswarick *Base Sculptor:* Paul Van Ommen *Painter:* Dordi Moen

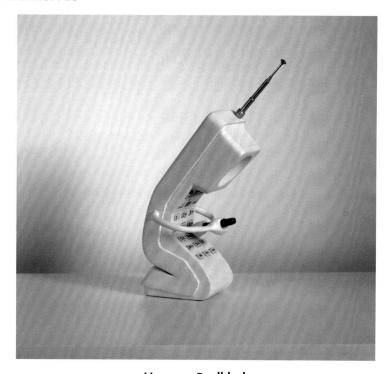

Maryam Dadkhah
Title: Seppuku *Medium:* Found objects and epoxy clay
Size: Base: 3 x 2.5 in., Height: 8 in. *Designer:* Maryam Dadkhah

Olivier Villoingt
Title: The Moon Keeper *Medium:* Monster clay *Size:* 4.25 x 8 in.

Valentin ZAK
Title: Weasel Riders *Medium:* Polymer clay (fimo) *Size:* 6 x 3.25 in. *Photographer:* Bear McGivney *Client:* Blacksmith Miniatures
Based on an artwork by Jean-Baptiste Monge

Colin and Kristine Poole
Title: The Flight of the Goddess Saga *Medium:* Bronze *Size:* 10 x 9 x 13.5 in.
Client: Denver Comic Con/Pop Culture Classroom *Art Director:* Illya Kowalchuk and Bruce MacIntosh *Designer:* Colin Poole

EDITORIAL GOLD AWARD

EDWARD KINSELLA III
MY WHEREABOUTS

Medium: Graphite, ink, gouache, and watercolor on paper
Size: 14 x 16.75 in. *Client:* Playboy Magazine *Art Director:* Chris Deacon

"Thank you so much for the award! I was quite shocked to receive it, and I am very grateful to have been selected. Thank you to the Spectrum 25 Jury, John Fleskes, Kathy Chu, the Fenners and everyone else involved in the Spectrum community. Thank you as well to my peers for pushing me to be better every day."

Edward Kinsella III is an award-winning Illustrator from St. Louis. His accolades include five medals from the Society of Illustrators and three medals from Spectrum. His clients Include *The New Yorker*, *Rolling Stone*, the Criterion Collection, *Reader's Digest*, *The Wall Street Journal*, the Folio Society, *Atlantic Monthly*, Playboy, Penguin, Simon & Schuster, the United States Postal Service, *Entertainment Weekly*, *Smithsonian Magazine*, *Wired*, *Texas Monthly*, *Nautilus Magazine*, *Scientific American*, *The Washington Post*, Scholastic, *The New York Times*, Houghton Mifflin Harcourt, *The Progressive*, *New York Magazine*, Sub Pop Records, Bloomberg Markets, Black Dragon Press and Mondo.

The Overlook Explodes

EDITORIAL SILVER AWARD

TIM O'BRIEN
"NOTHING TO SEE HERE"

Medium: Oil on board *Size:* 11 x 14 in. *Client:* Time *Art Director:* DW Pine

"It's a high honor to see the list of impressive jurors and all of the talented nominees and to just be one of the artists considered for this honor. About the artwork, Trump seems to offer unreal and fantastical analogies on a daily basis. Thanks to Spectrum for celebrating such a wide spectrum of art."

Tim O'Brien is a freelance illustrator, working since 1987. His realist art has appeared numerous times on the cover of *Time* magazine, *Der Spiegel, Rolling Stone, Mother Jones* and *Smithsonian* and has been featured in many other publications, such as *Esquire, GQ* and *National Geographic*. O'Brien has illustrated covers for most major book publishers (he illustrated the covers of the *Hunger Games* books) and has designed several U.S. postage stamps. He has received awards and recognitions from the Society of Illustrators, *Graphis* magazine, *Communication Arts* magazine, the Society of Publication Designers, American Illustration, Spectrum Fantastic Art and the Art Directors Club. He also received an honorary doctorate from the Lyme Academy of Fine Art in 2013. O'Brien's paintings hang in the National Portrait Gallery in Washington, D.C., and he was the recipient of the prestigious Hamilton King Award from the Society of Illustrators in 2009. For fifteen years, O'Brien has been an executive board member of the Society of Illustrators and is the current president of the organization. His numerous speaking engagements include dozens of colleges in the U.S. and overseas, and he lectured about his work at the United Nations in 2016. O'Brien has been an educator for almost thirty years and is currently a professor at Pratt Institute in Brooklyn.

Neanderthal Reimagined

Yoann Lossel

Title: The Rise *Medium:* Mixed media on Arches paper: graphite, gold leaf (24k), and silver leaf *Size:* 19.75 x 27.5 in.

Yuko Shimizu
Title: Unconventional Way *Medium:* Ink drawing with digital color *Client:* PLANSPONSOR *Art Director:* SooJin Buzelli

Victo Ngai

Victo Ngai
Title: How A Leopard Sheds its Spots *Medium:* Mixed media
Size: 8.75 x 11.5 in. *Client:* CIO|DI magazine *Art Director:* SooJin

Victo Ngai
Title: Sports Fans *Medium:* Mixed media
Size: 10.25 x 10.25 in. *Client:* Nautilus Magazine *Art Director:* Len Small

Cliff Nielsen

Title: Lord of Shadows: The Dark Artifices *Medium:* Digital *Size:* 9 x 11 in. *Client:* Margaret K. McElderry Books *Art Director:* Russell Gordon *Designer:* Cliff Nielsen

Shreya Gupta
Title: Confronting Sexual Harassment in Science   *Medium:* Ink, graphite and digital   *Size:* 12 x 8 in.   *Client:* Scientific American   *Art Director:* Michael Mrak

Cliff Nielsen
Title: Queen of Air and Darkness: The Dark Artifices
Medium: Digital   *Size:* 9 x 11 in.   *Client:* Margaret K. McElderry Books   *Art Director:* Russell Gordon   *Designer:* Cliff Nielsen

James Gurney
Title: Khaan Displaying *Medium:* Oil on board *Size:* 18 x 12 in. *Client:* National Wildlife Federation *Art Director:* John Gallagher *Designer:* Kathy Kranking

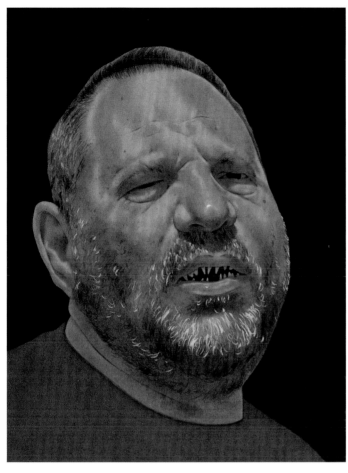

Edward Kinsella III
Title: Harvey Weinstein, Monster
Medium: Graphite, ink, gouache, and watercolor on paper *Size:* 5 x 6.5 in.
Client: The Hollywood Reporter *Art Director:* Shanti Marlar

Tim O'Brien
Title: "Trump's War on Washington" *Medium:* Oil on board
Size: 11 x 14 in. *Client:* Time *Art Director:* DW Pine

Taylor Wessling
Title: Prickly Priest *Medium:* Graphite, charcoal, acrylic, watercolor, ink and digital
Size: 6 x 8.75 in. *Client:* The Baffler *Art Director:* Lindsay Ballant

Craig Elliott
Title: Flooded Forest *Medium:* Digital *Size:* 25 x 16 in. *Client:* ImagineFX Magazine *Art Director:* Claire Howlett

Galen Dara
Title: Bear Language *Medium:* Digital *Size:* 10.5 x 6 in. *Client:* Fireside Magazine *Art Director:* Pablo Defendini

Donato Giancola
Title: Life Seeker *Medium:* Oil on panel *Size:* 48 x 36 in. *Client:* Asimov's SF

Micah Epstein
Title: Angel of the Blockade *Medium:* Pencil and digital
Size: 6.5 x 9.5 in. *Client:* Tor.com *Art Director:* Irene Gallo

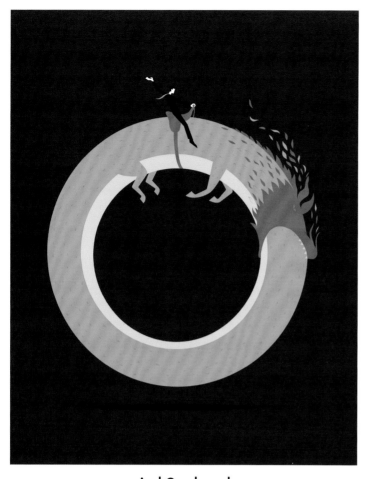

Aad Goudappel
Title: Magazine cover-Circulair Economy-Ouroboros
Medium: Digital *Size:* 9 x 11.5 in. *Client:* Managementboek Magazine
Art Director: Daan Zeijdner *Designer:* Daan Zeijdner

Bruce Jensen
Title: Alzheimer's Laboratory *Medium:* Digital *Client:* CBS News/60 Minutes

Keith Negley
Title: Detroit *Medium:* Mixed *Size:* 8 x 10 in.
Client: The New Yorker *Art Director:* Deanna Donegan

Goñi Montes
Title: Sergeant Pepper *Medium:* Digital *Size:* 10 x 16 in. *Client:* Rolling Stone *Art Director:* Mark Maltais

Sam Weber
Title: These Deathless Bones *Medium:* Oil on board *Size:* 11 x 14 in. *Client:* Tor.com *Art Director:* Irene Gallo

Kellan Jett
Title: Diplomacy Mills *Medium:* Digital *Client:* Slate *Art Director:* Lisa Larson-Walker

Leonardo Santamaria
Title: How First-Generation College Students Do Thanksgiving Break *Medium:* Acrylic, graphite, and colored pencil on paper, finished digitally
Size: 10.5 x 15.5 in. *Client:* The New York Times: Sunday Review *Art Director:* Nathan Huang

INSTITUTIONAL GOLD AWARD

SEB MCKINNON
STASIS

Medium: Digital *Size:* 11 x 8.25 in. *Client:* Magic: The Gathering *Art Director:* Dawn Murin

"When I was studying art in college, one of my teachers would bring the Spectrum books to class. A peculiar emotion stirred within me then—a deep desire to one day earn my place among those artists—and I've since given everything of myself to my work. To win this award means everything to me. A sense of validation that I am doing OK, that I'm doing all right. My heart holds so much gratitude toward the folks at Wizards of the Coast and to the Spectrum judges. I feel I am among giants, and I simply wish to continue doing what I'm doing now. Thank you!"

Seb McKinnon, the eldest of five brothers, grew up in the countryside outside Montreal. After graduating from the Illustration & Design program at Dawson College, he started working for Ubisoft as a concept artist. Now a freelancer, he works as an illustrator primarily for Magic: The Gathering. His other passion is filmmaking, and he runs a Montreal-based company called Five Knights Productions, shooting commercials, music videos and short films. For the past five years, McKinnon has been working on his own IP called KIN Fables, a cinematic fantasy story-world. With three short films under his belt—*KIN, Salvage* and *Requiem*—McKinnon is set to direct his debut feature film, taking place in the KIN Fables universe. He also composes and produces the music for the project under the name Clann.

The Faerie Child

INSTITUTIONAL SILVER AWARD

PIOTR JABŁOŃSKI
MOANING WALL

Medium: Digital *Size:* 11 x 8.25 in. *Client:* Magic: The Gathering *Art Director:* Cynthia Sheppard

"This award was a bit of a surprise for me. Mostly because I didn't send any work for Spectrum. So you can easily imagine my amazement when I saw my artwork on the list of nominees. Quickly I got the answer that my work was sent by Wizards of the Coast, which I'm really grateful for. Of course this award means a lot to me. I planned to take part in Spectrum all the time, but I always thought that it's too early. Maybe in the next year I will have better stuff? And I'm glad that finally someone did it for me. Thanks!"

Piotr Jabłoński is a painter, illustrator and concept artist based in Bialystok, Poland. He graduated from the architecture department of the Technical University of Bialystok. At first he was interested in graffiti and street art, but after that he found out about digital art and was infatuated by it. His clients include Bungie, Arkane Studios, Aaron Sims Creative, Wizards of the Coast, Games Workshop, Platige Image, Applibot, NetEase Games, Tokkun Studio, Aggressive TV and Centipede Press.

Photo by LMFOTO   Referee

Victo Ngai

Title: Three Color Trilogy Blue *Medium*: Mixed Media *Size*: 18 x 27 in. *Client*: Black Dragon Press *Art Director*: James Park

Tianhua X

Title: Dinosaur Hunter *Medium:* Digital *Size:* 11 x 8.25 in. *Client:* Magic: The Gathering *Art Director:* Dawn Murin

Chris Rahn
Title: Vraska, Relic Seeker *Medium:* Traditional *Size:* 11.25 x 15 in. *Client:* Magic: The Gathering *Art Director:* Cynthia Sheppard

Chris Rahn
Title: Trapjaw Tyrant *Medium:* Traditional *Size:* 11 x 8.25 in. *Client:* Magic: The Gathering *Art Director:* Dawn Murin

Chris Rahn
Title: Huatli, Radiant Champion
Medium: Traditional
Size: 11.25 x 15 in.
Client: Magic: The Gathering
Art Director: Dawn Murin

Piotr Jabłoński
Title: Apocalypse Demon *Medium:* Digital *Size:* 11 x 8.25 in. *Client:* Magic: The Gathering *Art Director:* Cynthia Sheppard

Seb McKinnon
Title: Cuombajj Witches *Medium:* Digital *Size:* 11 x 8.25 in. *Client:* Magic: The Gathering *Art Director:* Dawn Murin

Seb McKinnon
Title: Duskborne Skymarcher *Medium:* Digital *Size:* 11 x 8.25 in. *Client:* Magic: The Gathering *Art Director:* Dawn Murin

Alex Konstad
Title: River Heralds Boon *Medium:* Digital *Size:* 11 x 8.25 in. *Client:* Magic: The Gathering *Art Director:* Cynthia Sheppard

Chris Seaman
Title: Giltgrove Stalker *Medium:* Acrylic on board *Size:* 12 x 16 in.
Client: Wizards of the Coast *Art Director:* Dawn Murin *Designer:* Magic: The Gathering Rivals of Ixalan

Eric Deschamps
Title: Drover of the Mighty *Medium:* Digital *Size:* 17 x 13 in. *Client:* Wizards of the Coast *Art Director:* Cynthia Sheppard

Even Amundsen
Title: Squirrel-Powered Scheme *Medium:* Digital *Size:* 11 x 8.25 in. *Client:* Magic: The Gathering *Art Director:* Dawn Murin

Carmen Sinek
Title: Crashing Tide *Medium:* Digital *Size:* 8 x 6 in. *Client:* Wizards of the Coast *Art Director:* Cynthia Sheppard

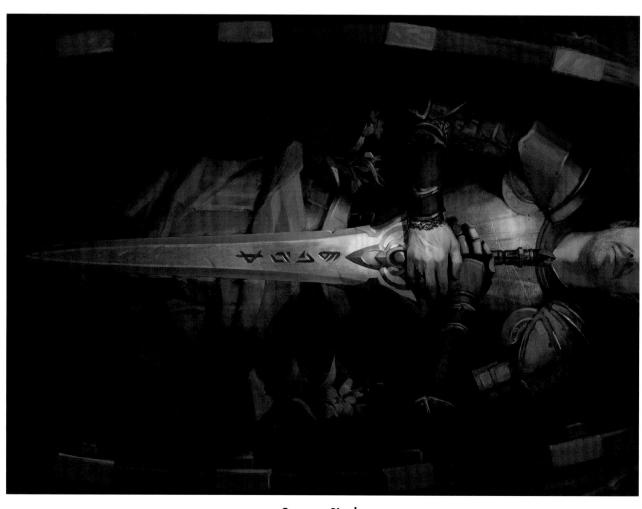

Carmen Sinek
Title: Heirloom Blade *Medium:* Digital *Size:* 8 x 6 in. *Client:* Wizards of the Coast *Art Director:* Mark Winters

James Ryman
Title: Aven of Enduring Hope *Medium:* Digital *Size:* 11 x 8.25 in. *Client:* Magic: The Gathering *Art Director:* Cynthia Sheppard

Jesper Ejsing
Title: Colossal Dreadmaw *Medium:* Acrylics *Size:* 16 x 12 in. *Client:* Wizards of the Coast *Art Director:* Dawn Murrin

Kieran Yanner
Title: Merfolk Branchwalker *Medium:* Digital *Size:* 16.75 x 12.25 in. *Client:* Magic: The Gathering *Art Director:* Dawn Murin

Lucas Graciano
Title: Pounce *Medium:* Oil *Size:* 18 x 24 in. *Client:* Wizards of the Coast *Art Director:* Dawn Murin

Lius Lasahido
Title: The Locust God *Medium:* Digital *Size:* 13.5 x 10 in. *Client:* Magic: The Gathering *Art Director:* Mark Winters

Marco Teixeira
Title: Clocknapper *Medium:* Digital *Size:* 11 x 8.25 in. *Client:* Magic: The Gathering *Art Director:* Dawn Murin

Mike Burns
Title: Party Crasher *Medium:* Photoshop *Client:* Wizards of the Coast *Art Director:* Dawn Murin

Raymond Swanland
Title: Etali, Primal Storm *Medium:* Digital *Size:* 13.5 x 10 in. *Client:* Magic: The Gathering *Art Director:* Cynthia Sheppard

Noah Bradley
Title: Doomsday *Medium:* Digital *Size:* 33 x 24 in. *Client:* Wizards of the Coast *Art Director:* Mark Winters

Randy Gallegos
Title: Inspiring Cleric *Medium:* Oil *Size:* 24 x 18 in. *Client:* Wizards of the Coast *Art Director:* Dawn Murin

Ryan Pancoast
Title: Deadeye Harpooner *Medium:* Oil on board *Size:* 14 x 18 in. *Client:* Wizards of the Coast *Art Director:* Cynthia Sheppard

Ryan Pancoast
Title: Ripjaw Raptor *Medium:* Oil on board *Size:* 12 x 16 in. *Client:* Wizards of the Coast *Art Director:* Cynthia Sheppard

Sidharth Chaturvedi
Title: Mighty Leap *Medium:* Digital *Client:* Wizards of the Coast *Art Director:* Mark Winters

Simon Dominic
Title: Dr. Julius Jumblemorph *Medium:* Digital *Size:* 11 x 8.25 in. *Client:* Magic: The Gathering *Art Director:* Dawn Murin

Slawomir Maniak
Title: Angel of Condemnation *Medium:* Digital *Size:* 26.75 x 19.5 in. *Client:* Magic: The Gathering *Art Director:* Mark Winters

Victor Maury
Title: Galio, the Colossus *Medium:* Digital *Size:* 27 x 12 in. *Client:* Riot Games *Art Director:* League of Legends Art Team ©Riot Games

Slawomir Maniak
Title: Silvergill Adept *Medium:* Digital *Size:* 23.25 x 31.75 in. *Client:* Magic: The Gathering *Art Director:* Dawn Murin

Wesley Burt
Title: Attune with Aether *Medium:* Digital *Size:* 10 x 14 in. *Client:* Wizards of the Coast *Art Director:* Dawn Murin, Cynthia Sheppard and Mark Winters

Zoltan Boros
Title: Frilled Deathspitter *Medium:* Digital *Size:* 11 x 8.25 in. *Client:* Magic: The Gathering *Art Director:* Cynthia Sheppard

Zoltan Boros
Title: Vault of Dragons *Medium:* Digital *Size:* 13 x 8 in. *Client:* Dungeons & Dragons/Wizards of the Coast *Art Director:* Shauna Narciso

Steve Prescott
Title: Contraptions: Goblin Explosioneers *Medium:* Acrylic *Size:* 23 x 32 in. *Client:* Magic: The Gathering *Art Director:* Dawn Murin

Ralph Horsley
Title: Contraptions: Agents of S.N.E.A.K. *Medium:* Oil *Size:* 26 x 35.5 in. *Client:* Magic: The Gathering *Art Director:* Dawn Murin

Andrew Sides
Title: Undertow *Medium:* Mixed media *Size:* 15 x 20 in.

Alix Branwyn
Title: Hexen: Memento Mori *Medium:* Digital *Size:* 12 x 18 in.

Te Hu
Title: Drum Clan *Medium:* Digital *Size:* 65 x 27 in. *Client:* Trojan Horse was a Unicorn

Alix Branwyn
Title: Hexen: Temptation *Medium:* Digital *Size:* 12 x 18 in. *Client:* ImagineFX *Art Director:* Clifford Hope

Sean Andrew Murray
Title: Gateway Uprising: The Fearless Four *Medium:* Pencil and digital *Client:* Fishwizard Games/CMON Global Limited

Thomas Haller Buchanan
Title: Madam Satan *Medium:* Mixed media *Size:* 13 x 16 in.
Client: PAJ Publishing *Art Director:* Thomas Haller Buchanan

Thomas Haller Buchanan
Title: Magic Rite of Drawing *Medium:* Mixed media *Size:* 13 x 19 in.
Client: Pictorial Arts Journal *Art Director:* Thomas Haller Buchanan

Terry Dodson
Title: San Diego 2017 *Medium:* Pencil and digital *Size:* 13 x 19 in.

Sean Andrew Murray
Title: Gateway Uprising: The Fishwife *Medium:* Pencil and digital
Client: Fishwizard Games/CMON Global Limited

Peter Diamond
Title: The Wind in The Willows *Medium:* Ink and digital
Size: 18 x 36 in. *Client:* Black Dragon Press *Art Director:* James Park

Russell Walks
Title: HOPE (for Carrie)
Medium: Mixed: digital, graphite, acrylic and colored pencil *Size:* 17 x 38 in.

Travis A. Louie
Title: Miss Calamity Jenkins *Medium:* Acrylic on board *Size:* 11 x 14 in. *Client:* Travis Louie Art

Allen Williams

Title: The Storms Lightning 3 *Medium:* Powdered graphite, pencil and oil on Ampersand claybord *Size:* 10 x 8 in. *Art Director:* Allen Williams *Designer:* Allen Williams

Othon Nikolaidis

Title: Conquest: The Exiles *Medium:* Digital *Size:* 40.75 x 47 in. *Client:* Para Bellum Wargames Ltd.

Allen Williams

Title: Divided We Stand *Medium:* Pencil with digital paint *Size:* 14 x 20 in. *Client:* Sideshow Collectibles: Court of the Dead *Art Director:* David Igo

Laurie Lee Brom
Title: Crystal Gazer *Medium:* Oil *Size:* 20 x 30 in. *Client:* Laurie Lee Brom

Tula Lotay
Title: Personal Shopper Mondo poster   *Medium:* Pentel brush and pen and photoshop   *Size:* 16 x 24 in.   *Client:* Mondo   *Art Director:* Jay Shaw

Bill Carman
Title: Panda Family Ties *Medium:* Acrylic *Size:* 8 x 10 in. *Client:* Gregg Spatz

Bill Carman
Title: Tigersnake *Size:* 8 x 10 in. *Client:* Jim Reid

Android Jones
Title: The Tower *Medium:* Digital painting
Size: 12 x 7.75 in. *Art Director:* Andrew Jones

Raoul Vitale
Title: Sepoy Rebellion *Medium:* Oils on hard board *Size:* 24 x 18 in. *Client:* Private Commission

Vanessa Lemen
Title: Harmony In The Ebb And Flow   *Medium:* Oil on panel   *Size:* 16 x 20 in.

Patrick Faricy
Title: Blood Rose   *Medium:* Digital, acrylic and gesso   *Size:* 11 x 15 in.
Client: Upper Deck   *Art Director:* Samantha Padilla and Jennifer Wu

Will Bullas
Title: Paradise...lost and found...
Medium: Watercolor
Size: 26 x 25.5 in.
Client: Carmel Art Association
Art Director: Will Bullas
Designer: Will Bullas

Brom
Title: Judgement *Medium:* Oil *Size:* 17 x 28 in. *Client:* Brom

Annie Stegg Gerard
Title: The Golden Lyre *Medium:* Oil on canvas *Size:* 18 x 24 in. *Art Director:* Justin Gerard

Sylvia Ritter
Title: The Lovers *Medium:* Digital

Alayna Danner
Title: Edge of Darkness Game Board *Medium:* Photoshop *Size:* 22 x 27 in.
Client: Alderac Entertainment Group

Paolo Rivera
Title: The Sinister Sixteen *Medium:* Gouache and acrylic *Size:* 19 x 25 in. *Client:* Grey Matter Art

Paolo Rivera
Title: Spider-Man/Venom/Carnage *Medium:* Gouache and acrylic *Size:* 14 x 20 in. *Client:* Sideshow Collectibles *Art Director:* David Igo

Cory Godbey
Title: Whence *Medium:* Graphite and digital *Size:* 18 x 22 in.

Donato Giancola
Title: Portal—Pathways *Medium:* Oil on panel *Size:* 16 x 20 in. *Client:* Abend Gallery

Donato Giancola
Title: The Fellowship in Hollin *Medium:* Oil on panel *Size:* 35 x 65 in. *Client:* BaltiCon

Donato Giancola
Title: Broken *Medium:* Oil on panel
Size: 24 x 18 in. *Client:* IX Arts

Ed Binkley
Title: Resurrectionist   *Medium:* Digital painting   *Size:* 19 x 15 in.

Justin Gerard
Title: Thrain at the Battle of Azaznulbizar
Medium: Graphite and digital   *Size:* 12 x 16 in.

Julie Bell
Title: Light From Her Eyes *Medium:* Oil on wood *Size:* 20 x 26 in. *Client:* Workman Publishing *Art Director:* Suzanne Rafer

UNPUBLISHED GOLD AWARD

ANDREW HEM
WHIRLPOOL

Medium: Acrylic on linen *Size:* 36 x 24 in.

"The award means a great deal to me. I've been a longtime supporter and follower of Spectrum, so I was overjoyed once I got news of winning gold."

Born during his parents' flight from Cambodia in the wake of the Khmer Rouge genocide, Andrew Hem grew up poised in the balance between two cultures—the rural animistic society of his Khmer ancestors and the dynamic urban arts of the tough Los Angeles neighborhood where his family eventually came to rest. Fascinated by graffiti at an early age, he honed his skills with graphics and composition on the walls of the city before following a passion for figure drawing to a degree in illustration from Art Center College of Design. Working in gouache, oil and acrylic, he weaves atmospheric, richly textured narratives in a vivid palette of twilight blues enlivened by swaths of deep red and splashes of golden light. His haunting impressions of culture and landscape evoke the life of the spirit through the visionary manifestation of memories and dreams.

Fallback

UNPUBLISHED SILVER AWARD

MICHAEL MACRAE
TIP OF THE SPEAR

Medium: Digital *Size:* 14 x 18 in.

"It's fantastic and humbling to be recognized alongside so many talented artists that I've looked up to over the years purchasing Spectrum books. I'd long hoped to claim even just a small corner somewhere in the back pages with one of my pieces, even if it were downsized into oblivion, just to say that I made it in this year. But what do you know? A nomination with a full-page spread? I'll take it. Thank you so much to Flesk, Spectrum, the judges and all the other artists who inspire on a daily basis."

Michael MacRae is a Vancouver-based digital artist working by day and painting by night, driven by the insatiable need to put his imagination to paper at the cost of all else. His illustrations vary from horrid darkness to the blissful expanse wherein he concocts worlds of mystery to escape to during the mundanity of everyday life.

MacRae hasn't worked in movies or on comic books or done much industry work of any kind, so he has been afforded the luxury of devoting the bulk of his creative energy into his personal work. With long-term goals of further developing his ideas into lusciously illustrated graphic novels, in the meantime he is content to just draw, paint and enjoy the creative process.

Iain McCaig
Title: Star Wars Triptych *Medium:* Traditional and digital *Size:* 35 x 16 in. *Client:* Lucasfilm Ltd

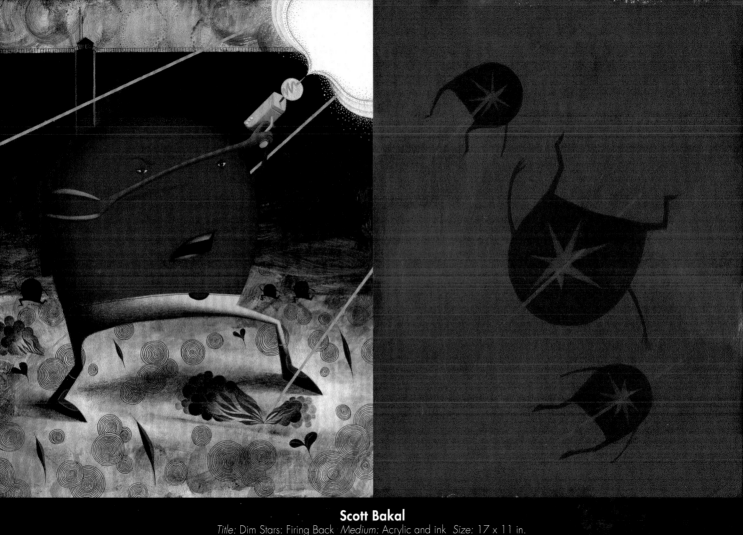

Scott Bakal
Title: Dim Stars: Firing Back *Medium:* Acrylic and ink *Size:* 17 x 11 in.

Howard Lyon
Title: Ella Standing Between the Earth and Sky *Medium*: Oil paint *Size*: 24 x 32 in.

Howard Lyon
Title: After the Dance *Medium:* Oil paint *Size:* 16 x 12 in.

Miranda Meeks
Title: Sacrifice *Medium:* Digital *Size:* 20 x 26 in. *Client:* Light Grey Art Lab

Jeffrey Alan Love
Title: War *Medium:* Acrylic and ink on paper *Size:* 12 x 9 in.

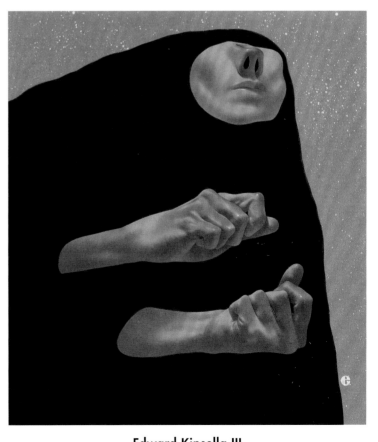

Miranda Meeks
Title: Hunger *Medium:* Digital

Edward Kinsella III
Title: The Creeper *Medium:* Graphite, ink, gouache, and watercolor on paper
Size: 9 x 10 in. *Client:* Nucleus Portland

239

Nicolas Delort
Title: Morning *Medium:* Ink on clayboard *Size:* 12 x 16 in.

Nicolas Delort
Title: Afternoon *Medium:* Ink on clayboard *Size:* 16 x 12 in.

Travis A. Louie
Title: Carswell The Magnificent *Medium:* Acrylic on board
Size: 11 x 14 in. *Client:* The Haven Gallery *Art Director:* Travis A. Louie

Rovina Cai
Title: Evening Stroll *Medium:* Pencil and digital *Size:* 8 x 11.75 in.

MJ Kim/Sewer Betta
Title: Eight of Swords *Medium:* Digital *Size:* 24 x 36 in.

Jumpei Umeki
Title: Pianist *Medium:* Digital and acrylic *Size:* 16.5 x 23.25 in.

Mark Zug
Title: Krypton *Medium:* Oil on canvas *Size:* 24 x 24 in.

Annie Stegg Gerard
Title: Ambiguous Thoughts/Halcyon Garden
Medium: Oil on canvas *Size:* 8 x 8 in. *Client:* Haven Gallery

Annie Stegg Gerard
Title: Sleeping Wishes/Halcyon Garden *Medium:* Oil on canvas *Client:* Haven Gallery

Cynthia Sheppard
Title: Deconstructing Wonderland *Medium:* Digital painting

Rob Rey
Title: Allegory of Nature *Medium:* Oil on panel *Size:* 6 x 8 in.

Thomas Fluharty
Title: The Pug of Frankenstein. *Medium:* Prismacolor 901 Indigo Bleu
Size: 13 x 19 in. *Client:* Star Gallery NYC

Torgeir Gran Fjereide
Title: Thor Slays the Serpent *Medium:* Digital

Bill Carman
Title: Long Neck Uukulele *Medium:* Mixed on mat board *Size:* 7 x 7 in.

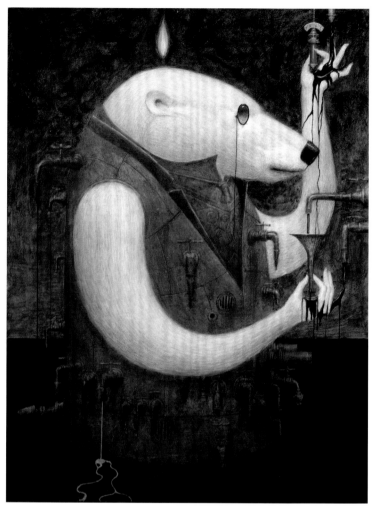

Bill Carman
Title: Goop *Medium:* Acrylic *Size:* 6 x 8 in.

Omar Rayyan
Title: Chickadees *Medium:* Oil on panel *Size:* 20 x 20 in.

Omar Rayyan
Title: Summer Beauty   *Medium:* Oil on panel   *Size:* 18 x 24 in.

Chris Dunn
Title: Carol Singing Mice *Medium:* Watercolour and gouache *Size:* 20 x 15 in. *Client:* Galerie Daniel Maghen *Art Director:* Olivier Souillÿ

Cleonique Hilsaca
Title: The Guide
Medium: Digital *Size:* 11 x 18 in.

Bobby Chiu
Title: Spring is Coming *Medium*: Digital *Size*: 7.5 x 9.25 in.

Emily Hare
Title: Howl *Medium:* Watercolour *Size:* 7.5 x 16 in.

Chie Yoshii
Title: Perfume *Medium:* Oil on wood panel *Size:* 23.75 x 11.75 in.

Chie Yoshii
Title: Deliverance *Medium:* Oil on canvas *Size:* 18 x 20 in.

Robbie Trevino
Title: Hill Folk *Medium:* Digital *Size:* 9.25 x 12 in.

Robbie Trevino

Top:
Title: Ritual
Medium: Digital
Size: 12 x 8.25 in.

Bottom:
Title: The Folk of Old
Medium: Digital
Size: 12 x 10 in.

Roberto Ribeiro Padula
Title: Pygmy Basilisk *Medium:* Photoshop *Size:* 18.75 x 12.75 in.

Roberto Ribeiro Padula
Title: Pale Strider *Medium:* Photoshop *Size:* 21.25 x 12.75 in.

Roberto Ribeiro Padula
Title: Rock-eater *Medium:* Photoshop *Size:* 12.5 x 13.25 in.

Antonio Javier Caparo
Title: Warmer Times *Medium:* Digital *Size:* 15.25 x 21.5 in.

Anna Dittmann
Title: Drift *Medium:* Digital *Size:* 22 x 13 in.

Anita Kunz
Title: DaVinci *Medium:* Acrylic *Size:* 30 x 40 in.

Othon Nikolaidis
Title: Man-Te-Pesh *Medium:* Digital *Size:* 8 x 12.5 in.

Scott M. Fischer
Title: Godiva   *Client:* GreenFisch Studio   *Art Director:* Teresa Fischer

Marc Scheff
Title: The American Dream
Medium: Gold leaf, mixed media, ArtResin on cradled board
Size: 18 x 24 x 5 in.   *Client:* Rehs Contemporary Gallery

Scott M. Fischer
Title: Of Wolves & Rabbits   *Client:* GreenFisch Studio   *Art Director:* Teresa Fischer

Scott M. Fischer
Title: Regal *Client:* GreenFisch Studio *Art Director:* Teresa Fischer

Steven Russell Black
Title: Inner Self *Medium:* Oil on masonite *Size:* 11 x 14 in. *Client:* Eileen Hendren *Art Director:* Eileen Hendren

Steven Russell Black
Title: Husk *Medium:* Prismacolor and charcoal on toned paper
Size: 11 x 17 in. *Client:* Every Day Original *Art Director:* Marc Scheff

Marcel Nowotny
Title: Captain at Night *Medium:* Digital

Allen Williams
Title: Hiraeth *Medium:* Powdered graphite and pencil on Ampersand claybord *Size:* 11 x 14 in. *Art Director:* Victoria Williams *Designer:* Allen Williams

Sija Hong
Title: Porcelain Pillows 4 *Medium:* Brush, ink and Adobe Photoshop *Size:* 20 x 14.75 in. *Client:* Tsinghua University Press

Qiuxin Mao
Title: Illusion *Medium:* Digital *Size:* 9 x 12.75 in. *Client:* SCAD class project
Art Director: Professor Charles Primeau *Designer:* Qiuxin Mao

Sija Hong
Title: Porcelain Pillows 1 *Medium:* Brush, ink and Adobe Photoshop
Size: 20 x 26.5 in. *Client:* Tsinghua University Press

Sija Hong
Title: Porcelain Pillows 3 *Medium:* Brush, ink and Adobe Photoshop *Size:* 20 x 28 in. *Client:* Tsinghua University Press

Tim O'Brien
Title: Trump Jenga *Medium:* Oil on board *Size:* 13 x 13 in.

Tim O'Brien
Title: Black Marilyn *Medium:* Oil on board *Size:* 15 x 19 in.

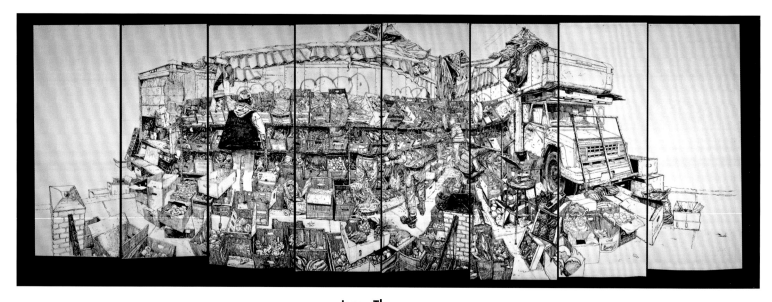

Jesse Thompson
Title: Fruit Sellers, Providence, RI and detail *Medium:* Chinese ink on paper *Size:* 288 x 96 in. *Art Director:* Jesse Thompson *Designer:* Jesse Thompson

Anthony Trujillo
Title: Alps *Medium:* Digital painting *Size:* 16 x 9 in.

Anthony Palumbo
Title: Searchers *Medium:* Oil *Size:* 14 x 11 in.

Justin Gerard
Title: Mean Tweets *Medium:* Oil on canvas *Size:* 12 x 16 in.

Rafal Wojtunik
Title: Return to the Family *Medium:* Digital *Size:* 20 x 10 in.

Kaitlin Brasfield
Title: Found One! *Medium:* Gouache and digital *Size:* 24 x 16 in.

Alex Dos Diaz
Title: Purge *Medium:* Procreate and photoshop *Size:* 12 x 18 in.

Ejiwa "Edge" Ebenebe
Title: Glimmer *Medium:* Digital *Size:* 13.5 x 20.25 in.

Ashly Lovett
Title: Eleionomae *Medium:* Chalk pastel *Size:* 9 x 12 in.

Alex Dos Diaz
Title: Hesitation—Awakening
Medium: Procreate and photoshop *Size:* 11 x 17 in.

Matthew G. Lewis
Title: Tukroun Konman *Medium:* Graphite and digital *Size:* 9 x 12 in.

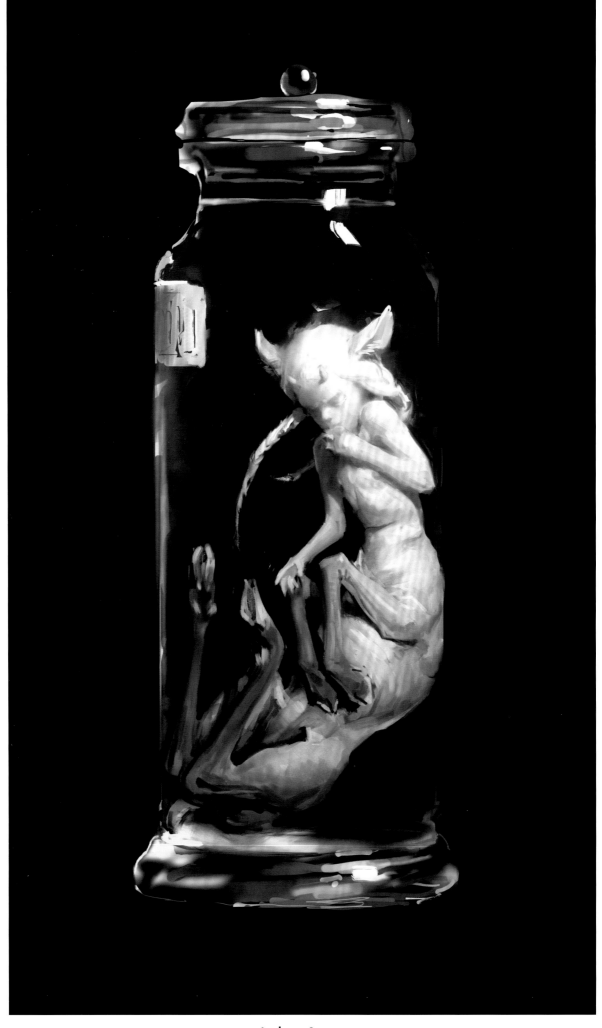

Andrew Sonea
Title: Deer Girl *Medium:* Digital

Jason Ward & Sheri Hansen
Title: Triassic Hunters *Medium:* Oil on canvas and Photoshop *Size:* 48 x 60 in.

Andrew Sonea
Title: Sneaky Gharial *Medium:* Digital

Das Pastoras
Title: Albino *Medium:* Watercolor
Size: 11 x 17 in. *Art Director:* José Villarrubia *Designer:* José Villarrubia

Daria Theodora
Title: Melancholic Shut-In *Medium:* Ink, watercolor and gouache *Size:* 9 x 13 in.

Neeraj Menon
Title: Qhel *Medium:* Digital *Size:* 8 x 12 in.

John Barry Ballaran
Title: Tundra Guard *Medium:* Digital *Size:* 9 x 12 in.

Daria Theodora
Title: Illusion of Safety *Medium:* Ink, watercolor and gouache *Size:* 8.5 x 11 in.

Allen Douglas
Title: Knotted Sawbill *Medium:* Oil on panel *Size:* 16 x 12 in. *Client:* Cryptid Visions

Jordan K. Walker
Title: Smaugust #30 *Medium:* Graphite on paper *Size:* 12 x 12 in.

Cam Floyd
Title: The Aviary *Medium:* Digital *Size:* 15.75 x 19 in.

Allen Douglas
Title: Bearded Fisher *Medium:* Oil on panel *Size:* 11 x 14 in. *Client:* Cryptid Visions

Alayna Danner
Title: Wind Vale *Medium:* Photoshop *Size:* 19 x 13 in.

Marcel Mercado
Title: The Call to Ruin *Medium:* Digital *Size:* 26 x 11 in.

Heather Theurer
Title: I Am *Medium:* Oil on panel *Size:* 36 x 60 in.

J.A.W. Cooper
Title: Festoon *Medium:* Graphite *Size:* 7 x 8.75 in.

J.A.W. Cooper
Title: Those That Trespass *Medium:* Graphite and digital *Size:* 13.5 x 20 in.

Ki "Gawki" Kline
Title: Breath *Medium:* Digital Painting *Size:* 13 x 19 in.

J.A.W. Cooper
Title: Sound The Alarm *Medium:* Acrylic *Size:* 12 x 16 in.

Jeremy Wilson
Title: Morte D'Arthur *Medium:* Oil on panel *Size:* 24 x 36 in.

Jeremy Wilson
Title: I Am Become Death *Medium:* Oil on panel *Size:* 24 x 30 in.

Jeremy Wilson
Title: Taxi! *Medium:* Oil on panel *Size:* 14 x 20 in.

Greg Ruth
Title: Lagoon 2
Medium: Graphite and digital
Size: 13 x 19 in.

Ahmed Eljohani AKA Eljo
Title: Breakout *Medium:* Digital *Size:* 20 x 11.25 in.

George Pratt
Title: Mary With Headress *Medium:* Digital, Procreate on iPad pro with Apple pencil *Size:* 13 x 13 in.

Kai Carpenter
Title: The Bonny Swan *Medium:* Oil paint *Size:* 54 x 30 in.

Maxim Kozhevnikov
Title: Honey Hunters *Medium:* 2D and 3D

Gina Matarazzo
Title: A Residence of Resonance *Medium:* Oil on panel *Size:* 8 x 10 in.

Lynn Chen
Title: Jet Corgi *Medium:* Digital *Size:* 10 x 10 in. *Art Director:* Jeremy Fenske

Tim Von Rueden
Title: Battered Bunnies *Medium:* Graphite and mixed media paper

Lisa Falkenstern
Title: Blast Off *Medium:* Oil on board
Size: 9 x 16 in. *Art Director:* Lisa Falkenstern

Lisa Falkenstern
Title: Pigs Fly Deux *Medium:* Oil on Masonite *Size:* 20 x 24 in. *Art Director:* Lisa Falkenstern

Camilla d'Errico
Title: Pop Goes The Weasel *Medium:* Oil On wood panel *Size:* 11 x 14 in.

THE TORTOISES

Carlyn Lim
Title: The Tortoises/Tortoise and Hare *Medium:* Digital *Size:* 12 x 5 in.
Client: Self/Artstation Challenge *Art Director:* Carlyn Lim *Designer:* Carlyn Lim

THE HARES

Carlyn Lim
Title: The Hares/Tortoise and Hare 2 *Medium:* Digital *Size:* 12 x 5 in.
Client: Self/Artstation Challenge *Art Director:* Carlyn Lim *Designer:* Carlyn Lim

Tom Herzberg
Title: Forget Me Not *Medium:* Acrylic on paper *Size:* 19.5 x 25.5 in.

Vojislav Nikcevic
Title: Ophelia *Medium:* Digital painting *Size:* 7.75 x 12 in.

Tu Qianwen
Title: The Five Deities *Medium:* Pencil and photoshop *Size:* 18 x 5 in. *Client:* class project-SCAD *Art Director:* Professor Mohamed Danawi *Designer:* Qianwen Tu

Chris Hong
Title: Naptime *Medium:* Watercolour *Size:* 9 x 12 in.

Caitlin Ono
Title: Paper Tigers *Medium:* Graphite with digital coloring *Size:* 17.5 x 11.5 in.

Isabella Kung
Title: Merbabies *Medium:* Watercolor and gouache on paper *Size:* 12 x 9 in.

Peter de Sève
Title: Small Fry *Medium:* Watercolor and ink *Size:* 10.5 x 13.5

Ruoxin Zhang
Title: Opal *Medium:* Photoshop *Size:* 82.5 x 53.25 in. *Client:* Ruoxin Zhang *Art Director:* Ruoxin Zhang *Designer:* Ruoxin Zhang

Ronan Le Fur, a.k.a Dofresh
Title: HPL was Right/The Sanatorium *Medium:* Digital

Shreya Gupta
Title: Based on Invisible Cities by Italo Calvino—Desires Are Now Memories (Isidora)
Medium: Ink, graphite and digital *Size:* 12.5 x 16 in.

Serena Malyon
Title: Erebor *Medium:* Watercolour and acryla gouache *Size:* 11.75 x 16.5 in.

Stephanie Law
Title: The Blue Above *Medium:* Watercolors and gold leaf *Size:* 10 x 18 in.

Rebecca Yanovskaya
Title: Paso Doble *Medium:* 24k Gold leaf and ballpoint pen *Size:* 12 x 12 in.

Kaitlund Zupanic
Title: The Harpy, Ascension of Hiraeth
Medium: Multimedia and digital *Size:* 10 x 20 in.

Joe Whyte
Title: Throne *Medium:* Ball point pen and photoshop *Size:* 11 x 27 in.

Sina Pakzad Kasra
Title: Joining the Party *Medium:* Digital *Size:* 20 x 24.75 in.

Bryan Mark Taylor
Title: Power Structure *Size:* 1.25 x 16 in.

Amir Zand (San)
Title: New Moon

Colleen Quint
Title: Meraki *Medium:* Digital *Size:* 8.5 x 12 in.

Ian Jun Wei Chiew
Title: Sanctuary I *Medium:* Digital *Size:* 23.25 x 11.75 in.

Donato Giancola
Title: Portal II *Medium:* Oil on panel *Size:* 24 x 36 in.

Djamila Knopf
Title: Ace of Wands *Medium:* Digital *Size:* 11.75 x 19.5 in.

David Brasgalla
Title: The Riddles of Gestumblindi *Medium:* Digital
Size: 8 x 10 in. *Art Director:* Gregory Manchess

David Vargo
Title: Wizard and Angel *Medium:* Oil on panel
Size: 16 x 20 in. *Art Director:* David Vargo

Inka Schulz
Title: Saunox Meadow *Medium:* Scratchboard *Size:* 9 x 11.75 in.

Julian Callos
Title: Déjà Vu
Medium: Acrylic and gouache on Rives BFK mounted on panel *Size:* 9 x 12 in.

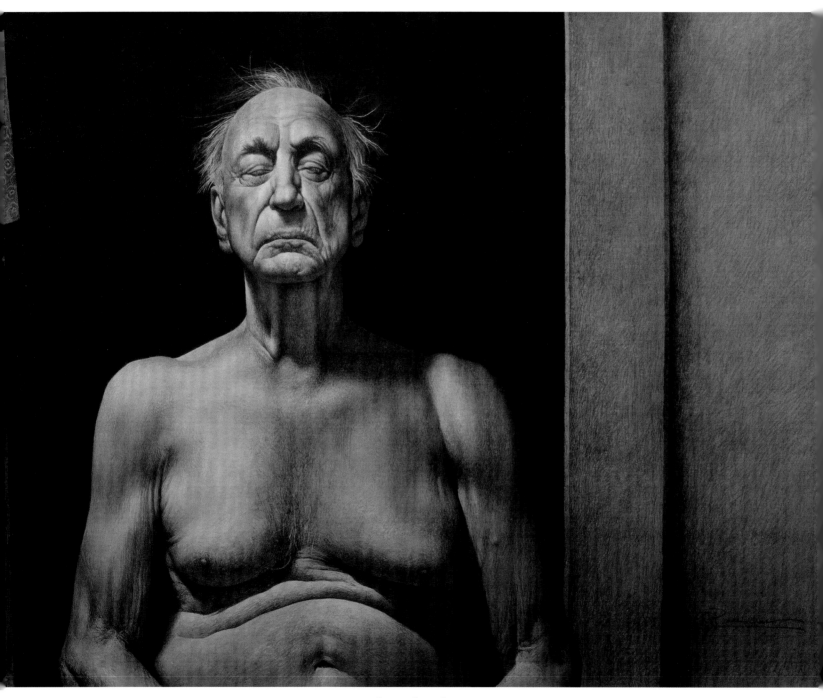

John Jude Palencar
Title: Centurion *Medium:* Watercolor, gesso and ink *Size:* 15.5 x 20 in.

Eric Velhagen
Title: Respite *Medium:* Oil on linen *Size:* 23.5 x 30 in.

ARTIST INDEX

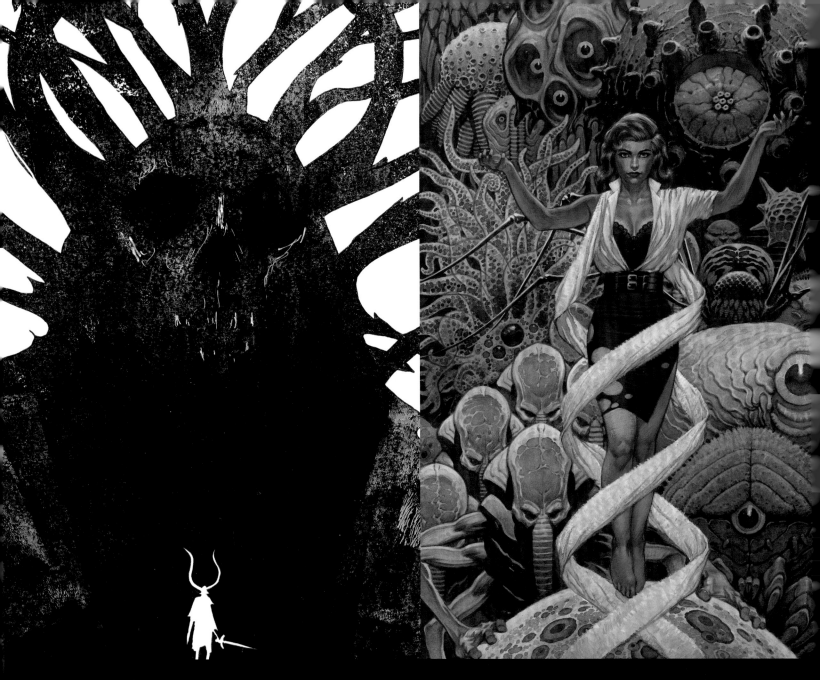

SPECTRUM 26

CALL FOR ENTRIES OCT. 15, 2018 TO Jan. 24, 2019

For twenty-five years the *Spectrum* annual has been a showcase for the best and brightest creators of fantastic art from around the globe. It serves as an invaluable resource book for art directors, art buyers, publishers and agents worldwide. Hundreds of copies are sent out *gratis* each year with the intent of generating additional work and exposure for the artists selected for inclusion in the annual. The circulation of *Spectrum* 25 far exceeds that of other annuals and resource books; we deliberately maintain a price that makes it affordable for every budget. Our purpose and singular agenda is the promotion of the art and the artists. We believe that *Spectrum* functions as a cost-efficient promotional forum and provides a bridge between creator, client and aficionado as well. *Spectrum* is all about facilitating opportunities for creators and about growing the audience for imaginative work in all its forms, without pretension and without prejudice.

The "Call for Entries" poster for the next *Spectrum* annual is by Tyler Jacobson. To learn more about *Spectrum* and for information about the "Call for Entries," please visit our website at *spectrumfantasticart.com*. The *Spectrum* 26 jury members will include Kei Acedera, Bobby Chiu, Edward

Kinsella III, and Colin and Kristine Poole.

Planet Comicon, one of the country's most popular pop-culture conventions, has announced that it will join forces with the preeminent fantasy-art show "Spectrum Fantastic Art Live" (SFAL) to create an unforgettable event. The show will take place March 29-31, 2019, at the Convention Center in Kansas City, Missouri. The all-star *Spectrum* 26 awards gala will be held Saturday, March 30, at the Folly Theater in Kansas City. Please visit *planetcomicon.com* and *spectrumfantasticartlive. com* for more details.

Flesk Publications works with dozens of today's premier artists to produce a full line of art books featuring the best of comics and graphic novels, fantasy, illustration and the fine arts. Our latest books highlight the works of J.A.W. Cooper, Gary Gianni, Jeffrey Alan Love, Tran Nguyen and Mark Schultz. Visit *fleskpublications.com* to learn more.

Left: *The Thousand Demon Tree*, by Jeffrey Alan Love. Right: *Carbon 3*, by Mark Schultz. Both titles are Fall 2018 releases from Flesk